DETROIT PUBLIC LIBRARY
3 5674 00581812 6
W9-BXF-571

Love from Elizabeth

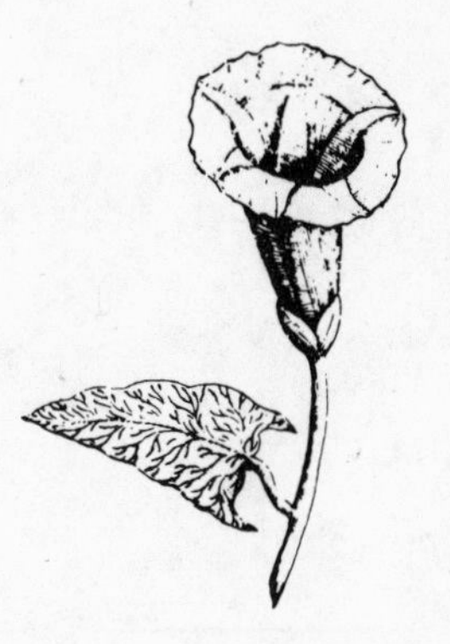

Love from Elizabeth

Meredith Gregg

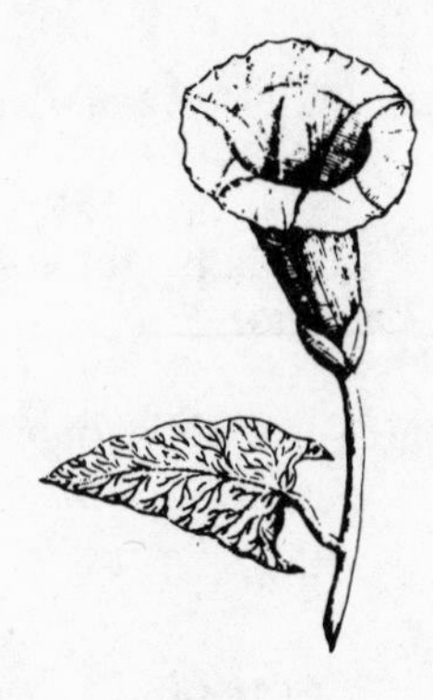

Walker and Company
New York

First published in the United States of America in 1986 by the Walker Publishing Company, Inc.

Published simultaneously in Canada by John Wiley & Sons Canada, Limited, Rexdale, Ontario.

Library of Congress Cataloging-in-Publication Data
Gregg, Meredith
Love from Elizabeth.

I. Title.
PS3557.R4334L6 1986 813′.54 85–26444
ISBN 0–8027–0875–7

Book Design by Irwin Wolf
Printed in the United States of America
10 9 8 7 6 5 4 3 2 1

Spirited Elizabeth Carlisle, 21 and not yet betrothed, and Giles Strickland appear always at odds in letters written by Elizabeth to her brother, Edward. However, Strickland does not take her tongue-lashings as affronts but is amused by them.

813

Dearest Brother,

The latest ship from America brought your letter telling of the burning of the city of Washington. What a sad end for the beautiful capital the Americans were only beginning to construct. You officers arrived at the White House in time to eat the dinner prepared for President Madison and his wife? I should have lost my appetite. Shame on General Ross for piling up the furniture to feed the flames. At least the men were disallowed to loot.

Our news, too, is of fire. Tonight the roof of the Ludlows' cottage at the south farm burned up. It was one of the first chill evenings; the Ludlows were burning brush since the winter wood supply is not yet stacked. When an ember landed on the thatch, the roof flamed up. No one was burned and only one man suffered injury: the man of business to Giles Strickland, Esquire. To *whom,* you ask? But I'll start at the beginning.

Uncle and I had been playing whist against Nan and Mama when Jem brought word of the fire. The Fates, because it was my birthday I suppose, were letting me and my partner trounce our opponents.

You can guess that Mama did not wish me to hurry to

the south farm. "Nan may go," she said to me, "as Jane Ludlow is her sister (Nan murmured incoherent thanks and hurriedly left the drawing room—if only she would forget just once that she is in service), but I think it more appropriate for you, Liza, to remain here."

"Liza may be needed there, Sister," Uncle said, pushing his own chair away from the card table. "I'll be escort for the two girls."

"I shall need you too, Liza," Mama protested, "to pour me a glass of ratafia."

Alas, our mother is all too capable of managing a decanter without any assistance from me. "Please, Mama," I begged. "The Ludlows have small children. And we do not know how serious the fire may be."

Mama waited an endless moment. "Well, I suppose if the children need you, you may go," she said finally. "But come to tell me as soon as all is safe."

Nan had already run to the stables to help Jem put horses to a carriage, so the three of us, with Jem as outrider, were shortly on our way to the south farm. Uncle had managed, I was surprised to see, to grab his sketch pad and paint box; I had not thought to bring even blankets or a bed wrench. And, of course, our scatterbrained Nan hadn't remembered her own bonnet, let alone emergency supplies.

You can picture the scene we found at the Ludlows': flames leaping from the roof, filling the sky with acrid smoke; constant hubbub of caution and advice as the Ludlows and their neighbours carted furnishings and foodstuffs to the far side of the dooryard; and the fire brigade swinging buckets of water up from the pond. Everyone was conscious of the danger to the cottage itself.

Peter Smith fortunately had assumed early direction of the effort to halt the blaze. While our tenants have begun to look to me since you took your commission, this was one problem another could handle better than I. My hands were full soothing the two children, who were on the verge of hysteria. Young Thomas sobbed uncontrollably as he pointed to the flames erupting from the corner of the attic where he sleeps.

The fire brigade had finally succeeded in confining the fire to the attic when a lone horseman gallopped down the lane. Where the road curved, the horse caught sight of the flames and reared in terror, flinging its rider to the ground. Missy and Thomas were shocked into silence as a second horseman pounded down the lane and wheeled to a stop by the thrown man. "Send someone for a doctor," he shouted as he dismounted. "And a boy after his horse." There was no question but that he expected instant obedience.

I called to Nan to take the children and hurried to the curve in the lane in time to hear the injured man say to his imperious friend, "It's my leg." Then he lost consciousness.

You can imagine the confusions of the next hour. (The danger over, Uncle ignored it all and tried to capture the scene in watercolour. I have not yet had the chance to see his sketches.) Instead of detailing the chaos, I will describe the two men for you. Giles Strickland, the one who took charge, is much the younger of the two: I would guess him in his early thirties. He has medium height and more rugged looks than convention deems handsome, although he carries himself as if he were an Adonis.

Daniel Rockingham, the man who was thrown, is as you will have guessed Mr. Strickland's man of business. He is no longer young; he must be Mama's age at least. Mr. Rockingham seems tall and good-looking, although of course I have seen him neither standing nor without pain.

Finally Mr. Rockingham lay asleep in the Ludlows' front room with the aid of laudanum. Those of us remaining—Jane and Edward Ludlow, Dr. Harrison, Uncle, Nan and me, besides Mr. Strickland—gathered in the kitchen, the room least affected by smoke and water.

"You're certain his leg will heal properly?" Mr. Strickland challenged. He paced as he spoke. "Should I not send for my London physician?"

I was offended. "Dr. Harrison is as skilled as any city doctor," I protested. I was about to launch into an account of your recovery from the carriage accident—my wretched temper again—when Dr. Harrison himself interrupted.

"The break seems a clean one," Dr. Harrison said. "I anticipate no problems. Although it goes without saying that he must not be moved immediately."

Nan started to ask a question but Mr. Strickland took the floor. "We are travelling to Lancastershire to my hunting box," he explained. "When my companion saw flames from the high road, he insisted on racing to the rescue. Although I assured him that—uh—farmers are best left to cope with their own difficulties."

Nan and the Ludlows tried to sink into their chairs. Uncle caught my eye to cut off a sharp retort and Dr. Harrison quickly changed the subject. "Were you about to say something, Nan?" he asked.

"I was hoping," she said in a tiny voice, "that Mr. Rockingham's leg will mend completely? He won't limp?"

You know that Nan has been one of the doctor's favourites since she came to us as the housekeeper's tiny daughter. "Nan, don't worry," he said. "He will be able to dance at your wedding."

Nan turned scarlet and looked to the floor.

Mr. Strickland stopped his pacing to gaze down at her from his eminence. "Don't worry, ma'am," he said. "Since my companion is my man of business, he needs his head more than he needs his leg while he is with me."

Nan seemed about to weep and I saw by the twinkle in Uncle's eye that he was about to make a reference to the "—uh—farmers," so I jumped into the conversation.

"Surely you will give Mr. Rockingham leave to heal," I said. It came out more sharply than I intended, and Mr. Strickland kept a keen eye on me as he resumed his pacing. I was glad Mama wasn't there.

"We must allow the Ludlows to retire," Dr. Harrison said to smooth things over yet again. "Why don't you all go on back to Strathamsford, Liza, and let me drive Mr. Strickland to the Rose and Crown?"

Jane Ludlow immediately offered their bedchamber to the visitor as Uncle simultaneously invited him to come home with us.

"I prefer to stay here," said Mr. Strickland authoritatively. (Does he think the Ludlows, being of the farmer class, will poison the broth?) And so we started back.

In the carriage Uncle prosed on about the fire and the strangers, his sketches rolled carefully in one corner of the forward seat. Nan huddled in the other corner and I fell into my regrettable habit of revising conversations:

Conversation revised

Mr. Strickland: He needs his head more than he needs his legs when he is with me.

Elizabeth: Surely a man of business needs a leg to stand on.

Mr. S: He is hardly on his last legs, Miss Carlisle.

E: I should hope not. He should be able to dance at *your* wedding.

Mr. S: I plan no wedding, ma'am. (In my imagination, I was dismayed to learn, Mr. Strickland is unmarried.) I am concerned only with the figure Mr. Rockingham cuts in his head.

E: Does he cut a figure, sir? I should think you would rather he increased it.

•••

Have you noticed that my revisions always seem to end to my advantage? And that others fade into the background of my cleverness? Please don't lecture me again. If I try to follow Mama's code of propriety when she can hear, surely I may suit my thoughts to myself.

At Strathamsford we found Mama still in the drawing room with her decanter. "Is the fire out?" she asked. "Is everyone safe? Was the damage great? Liza, your gown is filthy. And there is soot on your nose."

When she had run out of breath, we all tried to answer her questions at once. Mama simply seemed puzzled until we glanced at each other in the confusion and burst out laughing.

"It must be all right, then," Mama said. She turned to replace the decanter in the cabinet.

"Yes, it's all right," I agreed, and detailed for her the extent of damage to the cottage. "There was one injury," I began, but Uncle took up the story of the passersby and Mr. Rockingham's broken leg.

"Oh, no," Mama exclaimed. "The poor man. Dr. Harrison is satisfied? Maybe I should go right over. And strangers saw you with soot on your nose!" She looked at my offending feature with horror. I tried to wipe it clean with my handkerchief while Uncle calmed Mama.

"Everything is under control, Helen," Uncle said. "The Ludlows as well as their guests need to rest. We can call in a day or two."

Mama took a deep breath. "You're right, of course," she agreed. She paused as I signalled Nan my intention to retire. "The men," Mama went on. "Are they well-featured? Did they mention wives?"

"No, Mama," I said wryly. "Nor showed us miniatures of their children."

Uncle clucked. "You'll see for yourself very soon, my dear," he reassured Mama.

"Will you need me tonight, Mrs. Carlisle?" Nan asked.

"No, Nan," Mama said. "You're tired. Do whatever Liza requires and go on to bed." She sank onto the couch. "But make sure that her nose is its proper colour."

So she will wait to size up the strangers for herself.

Rascal is still angry with me for not allowing him to accompany us to the Ludlows'. When we let him out of the stables on our return, he greeted Nan and Uncle; but he pretended that he didn't see *me.* Honestly, Brother, you spoiled that dog terribly. Now he regards all excursions as his due. And if we had been on horseback he would have howled until we came home.

Nan and I spoke only briefly before I insisted that she retire. She was no more exhausted than I, but I determined to write to you before I extinguished my lamp.

We have had a variety of excitements for a calm fall evening. I wish you were here to share them, since they are, to the minds of a soldier's family, better excitements than those you are facing.

Stay safe and well and brave, so that England may win quickly and you can come home.

Your loving sister,
Elizabeth

P.S. The fire made me forget to tell you about my birthday and to thank you for my lovely little snuff box. I don't know whether or not to believe that Dolley Madison and her friends have made snuff the fashionable rage, but my box occupies a place of honour on my dressing table.

Do you believe that your little sister is in her twenty-first year? She doesn't.

Mama and I took breakfast this morning in her sitting room, of course, as we always do on my birthday. Poor Mama—her anxiety about my single state increases more rapidly than my age.

"Liza," she said, trying to look earnest while buttering a muffin, "a woman's greatest happiness is her husband and their children."

"For you, Mama, yes," I said. "But you were lucky enough to find Papa. Not all marriages are as happy as yours."

Mama's eyes clouded over. (Three years and still she thinks of him every hour.) "We were blessed," she said, remembering. Then she straightened her back. "But even a less happy union is preferable to becoming a spinster. Think of it, Liza. Do you wish to spend your life caring for your brother's children rather than your own?"

(Mama overlooks the fact that perhaps my brother—and his as yet unchosen wife—might prefer to care for their own children. Can you face me as Aunt Liza, always underfoot?)

"It has not come to that, Mama," I soothed. "My brother is yet unwed, and my hair still brown. When there are streaks of grey, I promise to worry."

"Jeremy Black will make someone a fine husband," Mama tried to sound casual and patted her own ungreyed hair.

"Ummm," I said noncommittally.

"If you should marry Jeremy," she went on, "you might always live near Strathamsford . . ." Her words trailed off and I know she was wishing you safe at home.

You *must* come home safely. Mama needs someone to tend, and surely you would not wish me the female fortunate enough to wed Jeremy Black. I don't think I could live with so much virtue.

I repeated the conversation for Nan while she was arranging my hair for dinner:

"Then Mama said, 'Do you wish to care for your brother's children rather than your own?' " I recounted. Then, "Ouch!" Nan had stuck a hairpin into my skull.

"I'm sorry," she said. "Maybe your brother's wife will wish to care for her own children."

"Exactly what I think," I agreed. "Mama still has hopes of my marrying Jeremy Black."

"That's not hope," Nan said. "That's desperation."

And, dear Brother, I am not desperate.

A summary of my other presents: Mama gave me a set of table linens for my hope chest. Nan embroidered a portfolio for my music (I must practise more diligently to be worthy of it). Uncle presented me with a small watercolour of a vase of daffodils. Will you be hurt if I admit that the painting is my favourite present?

Mama ordered Cook's special lemon cake for tea. If only you had been here, it would have been a perfect birthday. At least until its fiery conclusion.

I *must* go to bed.

E.

Friday, 1 October, 1813

Dearest Brother,

Everyone has had a busy two days trying to undo the fire's damage. Our tenants are working to repair the cottage roof: the framing and base are now up, so at least we need not dread rain. They will attach wooden shingles tomorrow. Jane Ludlow remains too frightened of fire to wish the roof rethatched.

The women, including Nan, of course, have cleaned the walls and floors of the entire cottage. What was not streaked with water was begrimed with smoke. Cook and I have fed everyone at huge tables outdoors, so each family had to feed only its stock at home. Fortunately the weather is fair and not unseasonably cold.

Dr. Harrison moved his patient yesterday morning to the Rose and Crown. I have had my hands full trying to match our pantry to menus for the crowd eating at the south farm. All the same, Mama insisted that I accompany her and Uncle this afternoon to see how Mr. Rockingham fares.

Little Becky Goodman, obviously feeling very important, met our carriage at the inn.

"Pleath come thith way, Mith Liza, Mithuth Carlisle," she instructed, as if we hadn't paid scores of visits to the

Rose and Crown. (I think she ignored Uncle because she never can remember his name.) Becky ushered us all into the sitting room, where we found Mr. Rockingham, his leg encumbered by a fat plaster cast. At least it looked fat under the coverlet; of course his breeches would not fit over it, and so he was in deshabille. His friend, Mr. Strickland, came to greet us and acted—you will not be surprised to learn—quite the lord of the manor.

Mr. Rockingham seemed glad to see us and not in any acute discomfort. His speech was slow, undoubtedly from whatever potion Dr. Harrison had prepared for him. Mostly he simply smiled in the direction of whoever was speaking. It was left to the rest of us to keep the conversation bubbling, which of course is Mama's element.

"Tell me, Mr. Strickland," she asked, "have you been able to notify Mr. Rockingham's family? His wife, certainly?" Sly Mama.

"He has no wife, ma'am," Mr. Strickland answered. He sounded bored, as if he were accustomed to interrogation from hopeful mothers. Not that I can imagine why any woman would wish to sacrifice her daughter to such arrogance. "His parents are at present in London," he continued. "I sent a letter by post chaise yesterday morning, to which he was well enough to add a sentence or two. I trust they will not worry."

"Indeed it is to be hoped they will not," Uncle said. "The solicitude of one's family can serve only to make one's misery general."

I wanted to hug him, but of course I could not do so in the presence of company. Mr. Strickland looked at Uncle with more interest than he had shown heretofore, but Mama would not allow a pensive remark in social exchange.

"I would be privileged to give them an observer's reassurances, if you will but give me their direction," she trilled. Mr. Rockingham smiled dully toward Mama.

"There is no need, ma'am," Mr. Strickland said condescendingly. "Dr. Harrison included a note to them in my packet."

I was relishing what I would say to him if Mama were not there when Mr. Goodman came in to offer refreshment. While Mama was occupied ordering sherry for herself and the patient, Mr. Strickland addressed Uncle. "I hope your other young lady suffered no ill affects from the fire?" he asked. "She is not with you this afternoon."

I interrupted to answer his question before Uncle could explain, even though I could feel Mama's eyes on me. "She is writing letters and begs to be excused," I said. There is no need for this man to know as much as he thinks he does. "Several men from this county, including my brother, are fighting in the Americas. We try to send messages with each ship that leaves to provision them," I concluded.

Even though I did not mention that I too had pressing obligations at home, Mama obviously thought my remarks as inappropriate as Uncle's earlier one.

"Nan is such a devoted girl," Mama said, reclaiming control of the conversation. "I shall insist that she join us on Monday for a harvest picnic." Mama looked beguilingly at Mr. Strickland. "May we count on you to join us while your friend rests for several hours?" One of the advantages of having a young and still beautiful mother is that I could learn so much from her, if only what she has to teach were what I wish to study.

Both visitors looked at Mama, one appreciatively and one cautiously. "Do come, sir," Uncle urged. "My sister's picnics are vastly amusing."

Mr. Rockingham said thickly, "Do go, Giles." He stopped to consider his next sentence, and Mr. Strickland interrupted.

"Nonsense, Dan," he said firmly. "I'll go nowhere as long as you must stay cooped up here."

Mama ignored the slur on the Rose and Crown's hospitality. "Very well," she said with a ripple of laughter.

"We'll bring the picnic to you. Tom Goodman will have no objection, I'm sure. Shall we come for luncheon? About one o'clock?"

So it was settled that we will give a picnic on Monday at the Rose and Crown. Mama looked pleased with herself for snagging at least one eligible man for an afternoon with her exasperating daughter. Mr. Strickland seemed suddenly very tired. Mr. Rockingham beamed at me, although I am uncertain about the sharpness of his vision.

I was about to try to get back into Mama's good graces by forcing myself to smile at Mr. Strickland when he quietly asked me a question. "You have a brother fighting in the Americas, Miss Carlisle? What is his division?"

"He is with the * * * *, sir," I said. "He served under General Ross at the capture of Washington City."

"My cousin is with Admiral Cockburn there," Mr. Strickland began to tell me, but Mama cut him off with a hand on his sleeve.

"Mercy, what do women know of war?" she said with a charming grimace. "A woman's job is to make a man comfortable. Doesn't your wife agree, Mr. Strickland?"

"I too am unmarried, ma'am," he said. He flicked his eyebrow at Mr. Rockingham, but his friend did not see.

Having not only found out what she wished to know but also set a firm engagement for the future, Mama finished her sherry. Then she declared that we must not overtire the patient and engineered a speedy departure.

Oh, Brother, sometimes I wish Mama weren't so obviously single-minded!

Conversation revised

Mama: Doesn't your wife agree, Mr. Strickland?
Mr. Strickland (to Elizabeth): Not very subtle, your mother.
Elizabeth: I fear she is not, sir. She may know nothing of

war, but she is a superior strategist in the battle between the sexes.

Mr. S: Or in the world of business, ma'am. I see her as a broker on the marriage mart.

E (defensive): Not business, sir. Rather I think of her as a devotee of the hunt.

Mr. S: That is apt, Miss Carlisle. But it is uncomfortable to be the prey.

E: Indeed, sir. Yet it is still worse to be the prize.

It seems, Brother, that I am becoming well acquainted with Mr. Strickland in my imagination. While I am sure that Mama will haunt both men with my company until Mr. Rockingham is well enough to continue his journey, she will also chaperone our meetings to make certain that I am eternally demure. How does a woman promise to spend her life with a man who knows her not at all? I suppose I do not have any truer idea of the men who call on me. But at least you, being male, get out from under Mama's loving gaze.

You may delete the previous paragraph. It is unfeeling of me to invent problems for myself when others around me seem genuinely unhappy.

We have been a sad lot since you went away. Uncle has not regained the exuberance he lost during his attack of ague in the summer. I think he is feeling his age.

I am concerned too about Nan. Her mind is elsewhere much of the time—you can guess she is more scatter-brained than ever. She spends many hours "writing letters." She receives no replies here, but she makes trips to the village for the flimsiest reasons. I offered to walk with her this morning, for example, because I needed writing paper, but she insisted on getting it in my place.

What if Nan has formed an attachment for someone unsuitable? Why else would she not tell me? If she should wish to marry him, how would I—or any of us—get along without her?

Of course there is nothing you can say in answer to the preceding question. There is something you can do, however, to help Mama. Please try to write to her more often. I know it is difficult for you to keep materials for correspondence, let alone to find time to write and means of transmittal. But she worries about you so, and sometimes finds solace in her decanter, which worries the rest of us. If it is at all possible, could you reassure her?

But don't neglect

Your loving sister,
Elizabeth

Saturday, 2 October, 1813

Dearest Brother,

How are you? I try to picture where you are and what you are doing, but it is hopeless. I pray that you are safe and comfortable, and that this awful war is soon over.

Our week has been frantically busy. The clean-up and repair from last week's fire—on top of the harvesting—have occupied everyone old enough to help. As a result, Mama has had no one to direct in digging up her Holland bulbs for winter. Except for her fumble-fingers daughter. Oh, Brother, I can hear you laughing. And it was even funnier than you imagine.

This morning Nan and I were sharing an early breakfast before she left to join those at the Ludlows', when who should walk into the breakfast room but Mama. I nearly choked on my tea. She has not risen before eight o'clock since the day you left.

"Are you well, Mama?" I asked hurriedly. "Would you like a powder?"

"I'm very well, thank-you," Mama answered. "Good morning, Nan." Nan smiled and returned her greeting. "But yes, I need you, Liza," she said to me.

"What shall I do?" I asked. "I'm hoping to join Nan at the cottage after I finish—"

"I require your assistance this morning," she said decisively. "I think we must get the bulbs up before the season is any more advanced. Jem did it last year, but he is needed at the south farm."

Nan and I exchanged looks. "Jane can manage without me," Nan said. "I'll take care of the bulbs, Mrs. Carlisle."

"Nonsense!" Mama and I said in unison.

"No," Mama went on, "you go to your sister. Liza is always telling me she will learn about gardening later." She gave me a look that challenged me to disagree with her. "Later has arrived," she ended triumphantly.

Of course she's right, Brother. I didn't know a Holland bulb from a potato. And if truth be told, I didn't want to know. But sometimes one learns in spite of oneself. I made the smallest attempt to postpone my dirty assignment.

"Your picnic is day after tomorrow, Mama," I reminded her. "I really must meet with Cook to finish the plans."

"We can do it in the garden," Mama brushed off my objection. "I have ideas of my own for the picnic." She peered at my plate. "You've finished breakfast, Liza. Now go change into an old gown while I drink my coffee."

"Yes, Mama," I said with resignation. I pushed back my chair.

"Shall I help you dress?" Nan asked sympathetically. She, too, got up from the table.

"Do you have a special coiffure for a morning in the garden?" I asked Nan. She stifled a giggle.

"Oh, I think a kerchief over your hair would be better, Liza," Mama answered for her.

"Then I can manage for myself, Nan," I admitted. "Thank-you anyway." I gave Nan a conspiratorial smile and hugged Mama's shoulders. "I'll be down shortly, Mama," I said as Nan and I left the breakfast room.

And so it was that I learned the difference between a potato and a Holland bulb.

"Gently, Liza. *Gently,*" Mama was saying half an hour later as she and Rascal watched me pull a bulb from the flower beds which line our lane. "It is alive, you know." She thought for a moment. "At least it was alive before you attacked it."

I grimaced and began to wield my trowel with infinite care. I gingerly loosened the soil around the next bulb and tenderly lifted it into the cart. Then I looked to Mama for approval.

"That's very fine," she said. "Except that it's also very slow." We both glanced down the flower beds stretching all the way to the house.

"I'm sure to get faster, Mama," I said, as I dug around the next bulb, trying to combine speed with caution. But just as I spoke, I stuck the tip of the trowel into the Holland bulb.

"Work as slowly as you need to, Liza," Mama said, suppressing a sympathetic cry of pain. "I'll change my gown and come back to work with you." She started for the house. "Remember: gentle," she called back.

"Yes, Mama," I said.

I had dug my way another half dozen feet toward the house—the cart was filling up with clumps of dirt—when I heard a horseman on the road coming from the village. Happy for an excuse to stretch my back, I sat up on my haunches to see who would cross the gap in the hedgerow.

As the rider reached the gap, he pulled up his horse to look curiously down our lane. He seemed as startled to see someone there as I was to realise that the rider was none other than Mr. Strickland. Your watchdog lifted his head and flopped his tail.

"Good day, ma'am," he said, lifting his hat. He spurred his horse to continue down the road.

I pulled the kerchief from my head and shook out my hair. "Good day, Mr. Strickland," I replied.

He jerked his horse to a second halt. "Miss Carlisle?" he said in disbelief. "Is it Miss Carlisle?"

"Welcome to Strathamsford, sir," I said, putting down my trowel. I stood to greet him. "How does your friend fare today?"

"He is much improved," Mr. Strickland answered, his mind obviously elsewhere. "He is not so heavily drugged."

"That is good news, sir," I said. "Will you come in for some refreshment?" I confess I hoped he could see I was not dressed to entertain.

"Thank-you, no," Mr. Strickland said, but he dismounted and stood next to me, holding his horse's reins. There was a pause. "You have no servants to do your gardening?" he asked.

"Indeed we do, sir," I answered. "But right now every hand that can be spared from the harvest is repairing the fire damage at our south farm."

"Of course," he said. "But is there no one to help you?"

"My mother is returning shortly," I replied in what I hoped was a final tone. "It is she who is eager to get the bulbs dug before winter."

"So that's it," he said. "You do not strike me somehow as the type to grub around the garden."

"You mistake me, sir," I announced, hiding my irritation. (You know what happens, Brother, when I lose my temper: my respect for the truth goes right out the window.) "Horticulture is my particular love," I lied haughtily. "But I defer to my mother's experience."

"I see," Mr. Strickland said.

"Pray, do not let me keep you, sir," I added. It's not that I wished to be rude, but can't you imagine Mama's reaction if she found me conversing with an unmarried man when I was wearing a dirty gown that Nan didn't bother to lengthen when I reached my current height? Rudeness was far preferable, as I'm sure you'll agree.

"Please give my regards to your mother, ma'am," he said, his foot in the stirrup to mount his horse.

"Thank-you, sir," I said. "I will." (Have you noticed how any lies after the first come more easily to the tongue?)

"Good day," Mr. Strickland swung his leg over the saddle and fit his other foot into its stirrup.

"Tell me, sir," I asked impetuously. "Your horse is a beauty. What is his name?"

"His name is Voyageur," he said, patting the horse's neck. I think he almost smiled. Then he and his magnificent animal continued down the road.

I was again painstakingly (and all too slowly) removing Holland bulbs while I revised our conversation in my head when Mama left the front door and started down the lane. As she came closer and I could see what she wore, I burst out laughing. One of Cook's aprons, which of course reached around her twice, was tied over a mourning gown so old she must have worn it for Grandmother.

"Oh, Mama," I cried, "you do not look like someone who would use the front door."

Mama looked down at the apron strings doubled around her waist and laughed too. She patted the huge white kerchief which completely hid her hair. "Yes, I know I'm a picture," she said. "Isn't it silly? I have nothing but kidskin gloves." She held out her hands, encased in black leather, for my inspection, before she reached into the apron pocket for a second trowel.

"Did Uncle see you?" I asked. "He would surely have insisted on sketching your costume."

"No, he did not," Mama said vehemently. "And I pray no one else will. How are you coming on? Your hair is uncovered."

I put my hand up to my head and remembered removing the scarf. I hoped I did not blush as I said to Mama, "What matter, if I wash my hair this afternoon." I busied myself with the next bulb and Mama walked on to the hedgerow to begin digging up the bulbs on the other side of the lane.

In what seemed like no time at all, Mama had come even with where I was digging tediously on. She came over to my side of the lane. "I'll work with you for a time," she offered. She watched closely as I pulled another bulb from the bed and placed it in the almost full cart. "You're doing well, Liza," she said approvingly. "I'll make a gardener of you yet."

"Thank-you, Mama," I said, stretching my back once again. "But you are the born gardener in this family."

Mama paused, her trowel in midair. "Don't you wish for a garden of your own, Liza?" she asked. "When I was your age, I had a husband and a baby, with another baby on the way."

"Yes, Mama," I said. This is a conversation we have had before. I have learned to ignore it.

"I can't understand why you don't fancy Jeremy Black," Mama continued. "He is quite the best-looking man in the county."

"Yes, Mama," I said.

"Perhaps you are attracted to one of the strangers?" Mama asked, trying to sound casual. "I'll write to my sister in town to find out more about them."

"Please don't, Mama," I said emphatically. "I have no wish to learn more about the men at the Rose and Crown."

"They seem more than pleasant to me," Mama commented. "The younger—is it Mr. Strickland?—acts a bit aloof."

"Arrogant is the word," I corrected. I jabbed the soil with my trowel, but Mama was thinking and did not see.

"Maybe you will like him better at the picnic," she said hopefully. "Do you plan to wear your olive gown? Or perhaps the burnt orange."

"Speaking of the picnic," I tried to deflect her, "what will we serve?"

"That's my surprise," Mama giggled like a schoolgirl. "Cook and I have planned the menu." I looked doubtful. "Oh, Liza, it will be such a feast!"

"Can't we take our usual picnic fare?" I asked. "Foods to eat with our fingers?"

Mama looked shocked. "These are *gentlemen,*" she reproved me.

"Of course they are," I agreed. "But surely even the haughty Mr. Strickland occasionally picks up a leg of chicken."

"The menu is complete," Mama said in a tone meant to forestall further discussion. She looked up from the bulbs and stretched her back as if it were aching as badly as mine. "But you'll help, won't you, Liza?" She didn't wait for an answer. "I *do* wish your brother were here."

"Yes, Mama," I said with more sincerity than I had given those words all morning. "So do I!"

And so we finished about a third the length of the lane. I asked for a luncheon tray in my room and I have just had the longest and hottest bath you can imagine. This letter is so many pages that my hair is already completely dry.

I just had a thought: isn't it lucky that Mr. Strickland did not ride back along the road while Mama was digging bulbs? She would have been mortified. I wonder where he was going.

I also wonder where you are going. Is it Baltimore, as the despatches indicate? I do so wish it were homeward. But perhaps soon. You are missed by your sister, who now has seen enough Holland bulbs never to confuse them with potatoes.

Love from
Elizabeth

Conversation revised

Mr. Strickland: You have no servants to do your gardening?

Elizabeth: Indeed we do, sir. But at the moment the—uh—farmers are busy coping with their own difficulties.

Mr. S: They certainly are not coping with yours. That gown is appalling.

E: It is suitable, sir, for grubbing around in the garden.

Mr. S: Is there no one to help you?

E: As you see, I have the cheering companionship of my brother's dog. (Pets Rascal.)

Mr. S: Hello, dog. Do you have a name?

E: His name is Rascal, sir. (Rascal jumps up on Mr. Strickland and leaves clumps of dirt on his jacket.)

Mr. S: His name, or his character?

E: Both, I confess. Now you, too, are dressed for grubbing around in the garden. Would you care to dig up a Holland bulb?

Mr. S: I'm sorry, ma'am, but I do not know a Holland bulb from a potato.

E: What a shame, sir. I have known the difference these two hours or more.

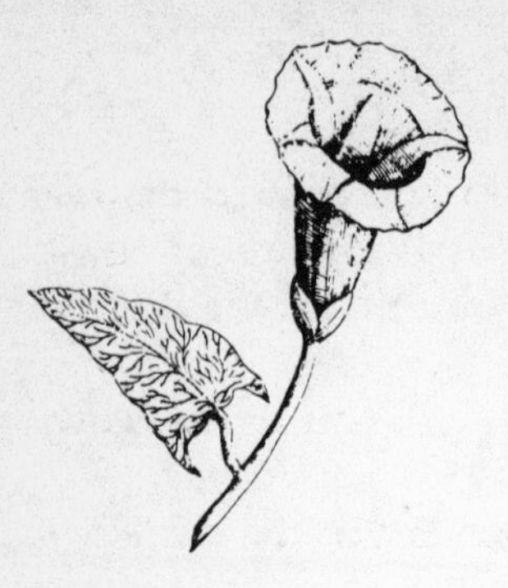

Sunday, 3 October, 1813

Dearest Brother,

How are you spending this lovely Sunday, I wonder? You must feel a long way from our quiet sabbaths.

Today, however, has been far from the usual Sunday calm at Strathamsford. We did not attend church, in the flurry of preparing for tomorrow's picnic, which Mama treats as if it were a banquet for the Prince Regent. Even Sunday dinner was nothing out of the ordinary, since Cook is gamely attempting to prepare all the dishes on Mama's elaborate menu.

There are problems. With the combination of complex procedures and necessary substitutions, the delicacies do not turn out quite as the original chef intended. Or what is more important, as Mama thinks they should. When a concoction obviously will not do—the spun sugar was a disaster—Mama searches out two new recipes to replace it. The kitchen is chaos.

There is good news though: I've been relieved of garden duty. Dr. Harrison is responsible. He called yesterday before dinner to report that the patient is doing even better than he had hoped. (I'm sure Mrs. Black would have been here long since to check the accuracy of her information about both the fire and the strangers at the inn, but the Blacks are spending a fortnight with the vicar's sister.) Mr. Rockingham is apparently a good deal more alert than when we saw him on Friday. The doctor said little about Mr. Strickland except that he is in the habit of taking a morning ride.

"He is?" Mama asked. She looked at me with shock. "What if he had chosen our road today?" She explained to Dr. Harrison. "All our tenants are busy, so Liza and I spent the morning digging up Holland bulbs at the end of the lane."

Neither the doctor nor I said anything, so Mama continued. "I think we'll leave the rest until Jem can do them. Surely they'll be safe."

"Oh, certainly they will, Mama," I said gratefully. I arched my back in memory of the morning's pains. "My muscles are glad to hear it."

Dr. Harrison smiled sympathetically. "Do take a hot bath," he advised me. "You'll feel better."

"Yes, I did that immediately," I assured him. "See, now I can sit up straight." I squared my shoulders for his benefit.

"Liza, you exaggerate by half," Mama reproved me. "Have you noticed," she continued to the doctor, "how much more tiring a disliked task can be?"

"Indeed I have," Dr. Harrison agreed. "But I'll admit that I wouldn't have the energy to dig up more than three bulbs altogether." He winked at me and began his farewells.

So now Mama has decided that Mr. Strickland may call. Instead of helping with preparations for the picnic this morning, I dressed in supposedly casual elegance to wait in the drawing room for a visitor who has not come. I feel like a doll in a shop window. By threatening to ride out for the entire day, I coerced Mama into letting me spend the time on our estate accounts.

I regret to say that this tactic has backfired: my troubles with the ledgers have only added to my frustrations. So I have shoved them aside to write—again—to you. If only you had not been called up so quickly and could have given me more instruction . . .

While I waited at Strathamsford in all my finery, Uncle was the one who spoke with the gentleman in question. He—Uncle—has been reworking his sketches of the fire, and this morning he rode to the village to order paints from London. He happened to mention at luncheon that he had spoken with Mr. Strickland on the way to town, and Mama immediately subjected him to intense inquisition.

"What was Mr. Strickland doing there, James?" she asked.

"Exercising both his horse and himself, I presume," Uncle answered. He turned to me. "His mount is a prime example of horseflesh," he commented. I smiled.

"Did he ask after Elizabeth?" Mama pressed.

"He made an inquiry about our household."

"Did you mention Elizabeth in your reply?" Mama wouldn't give up.

"Yes, Uncle," I teased, "did you tell Mr. Strickland that Mama despairs of finding me a husband?"

"Why, no, Liza," Uncle said with a raised eyebrow. "Actually, I mentioned that we keep a bludgeon in the hall to keep your suitors at bay."

I giggled. "I fear Jeremy would blanch at the mention of competition, let alone the threat of violence," I said.

"You mean you haven't told him of the duke's daily orchids?" Uncle seemed intently concerned.

"Indeed not," I countered. "Nor of the colonel who at my brother's behest will offer me his medals when he returns to England."

Mama could stand no more. "Will you two never be serious?" she demanded. "Liza will have her London season when this wretched war is over and my son returns."

She spoke so fast she nearly stuttered. "But for the present the Fates have given us Mr. Rockingham and Mr. Strickland, and we must not spurn their advances."

"Advances, Mama?" I laughed. "One man breaks his leg and the other rides through the countryside. Whatever would you describe as a retreat?"

"Mr. Strickland was riding *away* from Strathamsford," Uncle said helpfully.

"Well, maybe it's better for you, James, if Elizabeth does not marry," Mama said, pretending to be disgusted. "Then she can keep house for you after the pair of you have driven me to Bedlam."

I moved to hug her as she stood to leave the dining room. "Now, Mama, you know that the only reason you might go to Bedlam is to visit the rest of us."

Uncle got up to escort her from the room. "Maybe we should pay this place a visit, if we all plan to reside there," he said.

Mama sniffed. "Perhaps I shall simply remarry," she said, trying to be haughty.

Uncle and I burst out laughing. "Please do," I said fondly. "If you can find anyone good enough for you." (Don't you wish so, Brother? She has been alone so long.)

"But then who would put up with us?" Uncle asked over his shoulder as he went with her into the hall. I beckoned him back with a tilt of my head; and when the door closed behind Mama, he rejoined me at the table.

"Don't tease me as you do Mama," I demanded. "Tell me about meeting Mr. Strickland."

"The young lady shows a keen interest in the stranger among us," Uncle said to the portrait of Grandfather over the dining room mantel. "I wonder why she neglected to encourage her mother's curiosity?"

"Come, Uncle," I wheedled. "We are seldom treated to the excitement of a stranger in Strathamsford. And you must admit that his colossal pride makes Mr. Strickland more interesting than most."

"Unquestionably," Uncle said.

"He's quicker witted than some."

"Undoubtedly," Uncle said.

"And he is not the least bit attracted to me."

"Assuredly," Uncle said.

I almost stamped my foot. "That's really most ungallant of you," I protested. "Must you agree with everything I say?"

"Must you believe everything *I* say?" Uncle said with a smile. He was quite pleased with himself.

"Let us begin anew," I said as carefully as to a slow-witted child. "Please, dear Uncle, describe for me your chance meeting with the friend of the man who lies in plaster at the Rose and Crown. Mr. Strickland, I believe his name is."

Uncle picked up the game at once. "The one who broke his leg at the fire?" he asked.

"Yes, that's the man I mean," I agreed.

"The doctor says he is doing well."

"His friend, Uncle. Tell me about meeting his friend."

"Well, dear niece," Uncle began, "I met the friend of the man who was injured at the fire on the way to the village this morning. I was on my way to the village to order some watercolours from London." He paused in what he fancied appeared as deep thought. "I sent for only two tubes of orange madder. Do you think I ought to have asked for three?"

"Uncle . . ." I said menacingly.

"Liza, Liza, there's not much to tell." Uncle reached for a cigar, as he has been doing lately if we two are alone after dining. "We had a pleasant if aimless chat until he asked several questions of frightening detail about the management of our estate. If only you had been there instead of I, he might have gotten some answers."

"Nobody gets answers lately," I said.

It is sad but true. Mr. Strickland, Mama, and I each get no answers from Uncle, and no one gets answers from you. (I didn't tell Uncle about seeing the man myself yesterday. I wonder why.)

But I love you, answers or no.

Elizabeth

P.S. One needn't ask why Mama has now decided that I am too much indoors. Nan and I were directed to take a walk toward the village before tea. But I will not be maneuvered as Aunt Charlotte does Cousin Clarissa, so we brought our letter boxes to the seat at the bottom of the garden. Don't tell.

E.

Monday, 4 October, 1813

Dearest Brother,

Today was Mama's famous picnic. I remember it as Mama's *infamous* picnic. Oh, Brother, I gave in to my dreadful temper! The only consolation is that Mama does not know. But let me begin at the beginning.

Did I mention to you that the Livingston children have had croup? Last night the two younger ones—especially baby Annie—were worse, and Alice was worn out from caring for them. Old Mrs. Acton and Dr. Harrison were tending Sarah Brown through a difficult labor, so Alice sent word to Strathamsford that she needed help.

Since Mama insists on considering me a gentlewoman of leisure, I did not bother her with the problem. Instead, after a private consultation with Nan, I pleaded a headache. Mama was eager for me to retire immediately, so that I might be fully recovered for her picnic. Then I slipped out through the kitchen garden and spent most of the night boiling water for the children's steam tents. Alice slept to be ready to continue in the morning.

As the sky lightened, the children finally fell asleep; and Dr. Harrison, who stopped by after delivering Sarah of a healthy boy, sent me home. I tiptoed through the kitchen on my way to bed just as Cook was building up the fire to complete preparations for Mama's moveable feast.

Forgive me for prosing on. I am exhausted. And I am trying to make excuses for inexcusable behaviour. If Mama knew the worst . . . I hate to think.

She had bustled into my chamber about 9:30 o'clock this morning and started pulling gowns from my clothes-press. I tried to appear concerned about my dress, though my head was heavy and my eyes burned for sleep. While I willed myself awake, Mama instructed Nan on the arrangement of my hair and thanked God for the brilliant day. And she gave me a stream of last-minute tutelage about my behaviour. I can remember nothing now except her caution about seeming too intelligent. In my weakened condition I merely smiled and agreed and seemed very stupid indeed. Mama must have had high hopes of me.

She finally bade me hurry and left to supervise loading the large coach with picnic foodstuffs; I whispered to Nan to inspect the lot after her, and was able at last to sip some coffee in solitude.

Mama's menu was a marvel. Cold dishes (Scotch salmon with dill sauce, cucumber mousse, chicken vinaigrette with Andalusian tomatoes, three salads and four cheeses and half a dozen fruits) and hot dishes (ragout of veal, baked ham, fillets of beef, vegetables in sauces) all with warming stoves and breads and sweets and napery and serving pieces—do you begin to see the scope of Mama's vision? Poor Rascal could not believe that all the good smells were leaving instead of arriving. (I slipped him a tidbit of baked ham.)

Forgive me for naming such dishes to one on soldier's rations. I did not think. But this is a snack compared to the banquet Mama will plan when you return home: that dinner will defy description.

I arrived at the kitchen in time to see that the major problem in loading the coach was getting platters away from Cook, who continued to add garnishes to each until Nan shut the covers on her hand. Mama fluttered about urging everyone to make haste and getting in the way, while Uncle pondered aloud about appropriate wines.

We reached the Rose and Crown only about forty minutes after our announced arrival time in spite of all, which of course is on time for Mama. Mr. Strickland strolled out to meet the coach, but little Becky scampered around him to reach us first. "Good day, Mith Liza, Mithuth Carlisle," she said politely. This time she nodded to Uncle. "He'th in the garden," she went on without waiting for our greetings.

She stopped cold as she caught sight of Nan. "Nannie!" she exclaimed. "*You* came to thith party?"

I shot a look at Mr. Strickland, who appeared quite interested in the exchange. However he said nothing to Mama or me beyond his hellos and fell into step beside Uncle on the path to the garden. Jem and the inn's servants were starting to carry our hampers to tables set up in the back. Nan said something low to Becky and moved to help, but Mama motioned her to join us; she took a deep breath and came up to walk with me.

Mr. Rockingham sat on a chaise longue bundled against the breeze; he seemed eager and happy to have visitors. Mama acted very much the hostess, fussing over Mr. Rockingham and worrying about the arrangements. After the flurry of greetings, she bustled off to oversee the unpacking of platters; since Uncle was conversing with Mr. Strickland, Nan and I took the seats next to Mr. Rockingham's chaise and I handed him my spray of brilliant maple leaves.

"Thank-you, Miss Carlisle," he said sweetly. "Please excuse me for not getting up."

I smiled. "I am glad to see you as what I assume is yourself, sir," I said. "When we called the end of last week, you were a study in retarded motion."

"Not to mention retarded thought," Mr. Rockingham agreed. He returned my smile as Uncle and Mr. Strickland approached us.

"He is not yet—may I use the word?—burning up the road," Mr. Strickland commented to Uncle.

"Perhaps another turn of phrase would be more felicitous," Uncle suggested.

"Is that an observation on my intellectual powers?" Mr. Rockingham asked his employer. "Or only a wish on your part?"

"It's the former," Mr. Strickland said affectionately, "if you believe the latter." He continued almost to himself, "Of course a good night's sleep would smarten us both . . ."

Preparations for the meal finally seemed complete. Mama crossed the lawn to join the party as Mr. Rockingham said, "Giles, you see you need not hesitate to go on to Lancastershire. My care could not be improved."

Mama nodded at me to prod me back into the conversation. As she wanted, I pretended to pout at Mr. Strickland. "Perhaps you find fault with our entertainments, sir," I said. "Tell me, what shall we plan to amuse you?"

Mama looked at me approvingly as Mr. Strickland touched his friend's shoulder in mute commiseration. His attention was clearly elsewhere as he said to me, "Your family is all that is hospitable, Miss Carlisle." He included Mama in his polite smile and she beamed with pleasure.

"We are ready now to ask you to sample our hospitality," Mama said. "Won't you choose what you wish from the buffet, Mr. Strickland? Let me fill a plate for you, Mr. Rockingham." She looked at him questioningly. "A little filet of beef?"

The picnic was underway. I yielded the chair by Mr. Rockingham to Mama, who brought him a tray full of the most delectable morsels; she explained or excused as he tasted each portion.

Nan and I had little choice but to take our trays to join Uncle and Mr. Strickland. As you know, Nan can hardly be induced to open her mouth in company. Although Mr. Strickland asked her several questions, she answered in monosyllables, which discouraged further enquiries on his part. Since the small amount of energy I had gained from my three hours' sleep was gone, I concentrated on staying awake and answered questions almost as briefly as Nan. Uncle and Mr. Strickland, who didn't seem all too alert himself, were forced to carry the conversation at our side of the garden.

Then Mama rang her bell to signal the servants to exchange the plates for dessert dishes. Automatically Nan jumped up to wait on us. I grabbed her arm to pull her back. Her tray hit Uncle's shoulder, and the jolt broke her wineglass at the stem. Mama and Mr. Rockingham interrupted their laughter at the noise, but I gestured across the way that all was well.

Nan, of course, was almost in tears; and little Becky, who had hovered near since our arrival, tried to comfort her. "Don't worry, Nannie," she whispered. "If the Carlislth turn you off, you can work at the Roeth and Crown."

"Excuse me, please," Nan murmured in a choked voice. She darted over to the serving table to pack away the meats and salads.

Mama also excused herself to superintend the serving of her special blackberry tart, so Mr. Rockingham was momentarily alone. Mr. Strickland left Uncle and me to go over to his friend.

Then—my hand is shaking as I write; surely you can tell it—there was one of those lulls that sometimes occur in a social gathering, and Mr. Strickland's quiet comment to the guest of honour pierced my exhaustion.

"This is a strange county, Dan," he said. "Apparently the gentry socialises with its servants."

Mr. Rockingham's reply was lost as the sounds of serving

and low converse resumed, but I heard Mr. Strickland's explanation: "I believe our fair companion is the Carlisles' maid."

Truly, Brother! Can you credit the arrogance of the man? If he is blind to the worth of those he considers beneath him, all the wit and rugged looks in the world will not make me admire him. As you can unfortunately imagine, my temper took over.

Since Mama and Nan were still engrossed in apportioning and topping the dessert, I ignored Uncle's restraining gesture and walked as quickly as could be unobtrusive to Mr. Rockingham and his disdainful employer.

"Nan Andrews serves me first, sir, as a treasured friend." I spoke under my breath before Mr. Rockingham could answer. "As I hope I also serve her."

Mr. Strickland looked surprised and Mr. Rockingham dismayed. The latter began to speak soothingly but I cut him off. "If you respect only those whose position is as high as yours, Mr. Strickland, the air at your lofty gatherings must be too thin to be nourishing."

"Perhaps, Miss Carlisle," Mr. Strickland finally forced a word in, "pure air is more easily breathed."

Mama was crossing the lawn with a tray of blackberry tart. "You may be right, sir," I said as quickly as quietly. "For those who are ill in body or in mind."

Mr. Strickland laughed out loud, but Mr. Rockingham looked less well himself as Mama handed him a dessert dish. "I hope this is to your liking," she said to Mr. Rockingham. "Nan will serve you in a moment, Mr. Strickland."

Mr. Strickland gave an I-told-you-so glance to his friend, who seemed relieved that Mama expected to rejoin him for the picnic's final course.

"Maybe Uncle might take me home, Mama," I said. "I find I am suffering from the headache."

"What a shame, dear," Mama said, genuinely distressed.

"Ask Cook to fix you some hot milk. I'm sure the gentlemen will excuse you."

Mr. Rockingham merely nodded. "Of course, Miss Carlisle," Mr. Strickland agreed all too quickly. "I hope a change of air proves beneficial."

Odious man!

Uncle knows my tempers well enough that he did not try to talk with me on the ride home. I pretended to doze, while in fact I was replaying the scene.

Conversation revised

Mr. Strickland: Our fair companion is the Carlisles' maid.

Elizabeth (sweetly): She serves me first, sir, as a treasured friend; so I hope I also serve her.

Mr. Rockingham: Your friendship would be a treasure beyond price, Miss Carlisle.

Mr. S: I do not mean, ma'am, to belittle your maid's position. (He smiles.) Life would be much less pleasant without staff belowstairs.

E: Indeed, sir. We might even be forced to serve our own dessert. (Takes dish of blackberry tart and overturns it in Mr. Strickland's lap.)

Ah, Brother. Even in my imagination I simply disgrace myself further.

When we arrived home I went straight to my chamber; I pretended to be napping when Mama came up later to see how I was. But instead I am writing to you.

Perhaps the most grievous effect of behaving badly is one's self-absorption. I have not even mentioned how much you are in my thoughts and how fervently I pray for your safety and the swift end to this encounter. Stay whole, dear brother.

And wish me better self-control. I can only hope that Mr. Rockingham improves so rapidly that they will soon be gone and I can avoid meeting them again.

With love from your repentant
Elizabeth

Later

Nan has just come in with astounding news. Mama has invited Mr. Rockingham with his friend here to Strathamsford to convalesce! I suppose I am well served. I had hoped never to meet him again, and now I shall be forced to chat with him over breakfast. I resolve yet another time never to lose my temper again!

E.

Tuesday, 5 October, 1813

Dearest Brother,

It seems like forever since we had a letter from you, and I have just realised that perhaps it is because so very much is happening here. Is that right? Do our letters seem infrequent because of your experiences between reading one and receiving the next? You must remember to tell me.

This morning's flurry was preparing rooms for our guests. When they arrived just before luncheon, I was as mannerly as Mama could wish. (You see, my good resolution holds firm.)

Mr. Strickland uses your chamber; and a bed has been set up for Mr. Rockingham in Papa's study, so that the doors to the terrace may be opened if the weather is fine. Because the two men took luncheon in the study, we gathered for the first time in midafternoon on the terrace.

Mr. Strickland's stickpin contained a diamond quite as big as my fingernail; I'm afraid I stared. My awe together with my resolute amiability convinced Mama to take advantage of my docility.

"Come tell Mr. Rockingham about the garden," she called to me. "Elizabeth helped to plan the flower beds, sir," she was saying not very truthfully to him, when Sally came to tell her that Mrs. Black and Jeremy had arrived, fresh from Exeter.

Mama gave me only the briefest glance before bidding Sally to show them to the terrace—she should have known that Mrs. Black would not be satisfied with others' reports about our visitors.

I will spare you an account of the conversation; actually I heard little of it because of Rascal's behaviour. Your dog had been excited about the arrival of Mr. Rockingham and Mr. Strickland; the addition of Mrs. Black and Jeremy threw him into a frenzy. I was forced to excuse myself almost immediately to escort him to the carriage house. (Truly, Brother, your Rascal can be a real nuisance, compounded by the fact that since you're not here, he minds me alone. If it suits him.)

Alas, Jeremy jumped up to accompany me. Can you guess what is coming? You're right: I was unable to head off his declaration still another time. I wish you were here to join Nan and me in dissecting the occasion. Of course we ought to be kind. But the man is his own greatest admirer. Did I tell you Mama has heard that he is being considered for a large parish in Devon? He is quite impressed with himself. But I digress.

You can picture the scene: Mama pretending that all families include huge unruly dogs and I trying to retain a shred of dignity while keeping a firm grip on his collar and Rascal determined to make it clear that he is not slinking off in disgrace. All the while Mrs. Black is chattering and Nan is looking stern to hide the twinkle in her eye and Jeremy is complimenting me on my gown so as to establish a romantic mood. You would have been mightily amused.

Once we left the sight of the company I gave Rascal a good swat and told him exactly what I thought. The dog had the grace to look embarrassed, while Jeremy seemed surprised that I could give any consideration to Rascal while I basked in the sunshine of his attention.

"You were in my thoughts while I visited in Exeter," he announced.

"That's very nice of you to say," I answered, tugging at Rascal's collar.

"And then I arrive home to find (sniff sniff) you had a fire while I was gone." He was obviously trying to be gentle with his reproof.

"We didn't intend to exclude you . . ." I started in exasperation.

"Of course you didn't, my dear," Jeremy interrupted kindly. "But if I had been here, I might (sniff sniff) have been able to spare you."

I said nothing and pulled Rascal a little faster. Jeremy always seems to mix condescension with his kindness and he has never noticed that it makes me angry.

He continued his train of thought, a frown creasing his handsome brow. "And now these men, of whom we know nothing, are guests in your home. I've decided it would be easier for you if you gained my (sniff sniff) formal protection," he said as if bestowing a great beneficence. "I'll speak to your uncle this afternoon about making our understanding official."

We had reached the carriage house, so I was able to collect my wits while I shoved Rascal inside, admonished him to hush up, and made sure the door was securely fastened behind me.

"You do me great honour," I began, just as Mama would have wished. We started to walk slowly back to the terrace and Jeremy smiled indulgently, well aware of the great honour he offered. "But, Jeremy, we have no understanding."

His fond expression cracked just a little.

I took a deep breath and continued. "I value and rely

on our friendship," I said earnestly. "But we have nothing deeper."

"You are young," he said soothingly. "And unawakened." He glanced around to see if anyone was in sight and I suddenly realised he meant to embrace me.

"No, Jeremy," I said quickly and firmly. "We should not suit."

He finally began to understand that I was rejecting what he considered an eagerly anticipated proposal. "I am not ill-favoured and I have excellent prospects," he said petulantly. "I would be an advantageous match for you even if you had other suitors."

I fear my mouth dropped open. Jeremy was oblivious as usual to my reaction while he turned the matter over in his mind. "You don't have another suitor, do you?" he asked in disbelief. I could practically hear the cogs turning in his head. "Is it one of those (sniff sniff) strange men who are staying with you now?" He was convincing himself. "It's the one with the diamond in his cravat, isn't it? I thought the size of the stone (sniff sniff) quite vulgar."

"No, Jeremy, no." I had to laugh. "My heart is yet untouched. You must find someone who believes that you are the most wonderful man living in England."

"You don't believe that," he said, resigned at last.

"No, Jeremy. I'm sorry."

"I don't know what Mother will say."

"She'll think you made a lucky escape from someone who didn't love you as she ought." I spoke so quietly that Jeremy had to lean toward me to hear: in spite of our snail's pace we had almost regained the terrace.

"You're sure?" he asked just as softly, as Mama called out to us.

"There you are," she trilled. She looked at me inquiringly. "Did you have a pleasant chat?"

"Yes, Mama," I fibbed. "Please excuse our rag-mannered

dog," I begged the company at large, trying to change the subject. "My brother spoiled him dreadfully."

"Oh, what do you hear from your brother?" asked Mrs. Black, and the conversation moved into safer channels. Shallower too, since we have heard so little. We're sorry to be impatient. It's simply that you are never far from our thoughts.

Thought certainly wasn't necessary to follow the conversation on our terrace. The talk flowed around and apart from the men, as it often does when Mama and Mrs. Black share a refreshment tray. Uncle and Mr. Rockingham exchanged a few words and Jeremy was forced to answer frequent questions and requests for confirmation from his mother, but Mr. Strickland stood by, speaking only when spoken to. That is, virtually not at all. Finally he addressed me.

"Your mother says you planned the garden, Miss Carlisle," he said.

"I gave her only minor assistance," I insisted. "My mother is too modest." I expected to add that no garden looks its best in early October, but Mr. Strickland interrupted.

"It is delightful," he declared. "Do you enjoy grubbing about?" he asked wickedly.

Mama broke off her smile to protest. "My daughter does not do her own gardening, sir," she said with the merest trace of irritation. "We have servants for that."

"Of course, ma'am," said Mr. Strickland smoothly. "The beds are extensive. Would you be willing to give me a tour of the gardens, Miss Carlisle?"

"It would be my pleasure, sir," I agreed, ever the gracious hostess when Mama is but two feet away. (I wish, dear Brother, that Uncle had sketched the expressions of those who watched me start my second trip of the afternoon through the gardens: Mama pleased, Mrs. Black concerned, Uncle amused, Jeremy a mixture of regret and I-told-you-so.

I started an inane recital of the summer colours of the gardens, since we were still within hearing of those who remained on the terrace.

"You speak in general terms, ma'am," Mr. Strickland said gravely. "I thought that horticulture was your particular love."

Annoyed at being found out, I said quickly, "I'm surprised you noticed, since you do not know a Holland bulb from a potato."

"Whatever gave you that idea?" Mr. Strickland looked at me with surprise. "I've experimented with many varieties of both."

That wretched revised conversation! I struggled to cover my confusion. "Now I have two reasons to beg your forgiveness," I said sincerely. We were finally out of earshot of the terrace. "I've been wanting to apologise for my great discourtesy yesterday."

"There is no need to apologise," Mr. Strickland said trying not to smile. "I was highly entertained." (There you have it: the total effect of my outburst on its object.) "But surely," he continued, "that is not what you most wish to say to me."

"No," I admitted, "actually it isn't."

"Well," he challenged.

I took a deep breath. "I've been wondering," I said without any veneer of politeness, "why you agreed to come to Strathamsford."

"Why should I not, Miss Carlisle?" Mr. Strickland asked.

"All you know of us is that we socialise with our servants, behave rudely to our guests, and give tours of dying gardens." I paused to catch my breath. "Why are you here?" I asked baldly.

"Your mother was insistent with her hospitality," he temporised.

"Come now, sir," I said sharply. "We both know that Mama is no match for you. Why are you here?" I repeated.

"Truthfully, it was because of your mother," Mr. Strickland said with every evidence of sincerity. "Not that I was unable to refuse her invitation. But I feel certain that Dan Rockingham will be made as comfortable as possible in her home."

"That goes without saying," I protested.

"Unfortunately, my dear, it does not," he contradicted. "The Rose and Crown is a convivial gathering spot for the whole countryside. I'm sure I would find it delightful under other circumstances, but at present it is more important that my friend be allowed a few nights of uninterrupted sleep."

I was contrite. "Of course, sir," I said. "I didn't think. You're very kind." You may guess I was discomposed.

"I'm not at all kind," Mr. Strickland corrected; "I'm tired." He hesitated a moment before going on. "You will learn as you know me better that I am very jealous of my rest."

"You turn selfishness into a virtue, sir," I commented.

"Do not draw conclusions on insufficient evidence," he warned. "You may not consider it a virtue when you desire my company between eleven o'clock and an hour after sunrise."

We had circled the garden and approached the party near the house; Uncle started out to meet us. "You are in no doubt that I will desire your company," I observed. "How do you turn conceit into a virtue?" I smiled sweetly at my companion, since Mama could see us.

Uncle was close enough to hear my last word. "You discuss virtue?" he asked devilishly as we paused at meeting. "I trust I have not missed your talk of vice."

"What could your niece know of vice, sir?" Mr. Strickland reproved. "She is but a country girl, and could hardly recognise what passes for wit in the city, let alone what passes for vice."

"You will learn, sir, as you know me better," I said, "that I am very jealous of my country life. The city may keep both its wit and its vices."

Mr. Strickland laughed out loud. Uncle looked puzzled as Mama hurried over to shepherd us back to the terrace. "Whatever are you speaking of?" she asked me. "It sounded as if you mentioned vice."

Jeremy joined us and came to stand by my side. "What could Elizabeth know of vice?" he asked in disbelief. "She is all that is (sniff sniff) sweet and good."

Mr. Strickland and I exchanged glances. "Just as I said," he whispered to me.

"You must have misunderstood, Mama," I said. I thought for a moment. "Perhaps you heard me say that the garden's beauty is the result of your good advice."

"Your daughter does not take enough credit for herself," Mr. Strickland added wickedly. "I found my tour highly diverting."

"We countrywomen are farmers at heart," I explained. "Simple, predictable—that's what pleases us."

"Whatever are you talking about, Elizabeth?" Mama asked, looking concerned as well as completely at sea.

"Is anything wrong?" Mrs. Black was eager to miss nothing; she met us as we climbed the steps to the terrace.

"Mr. Strickland and I were merely discussing the satisfactions of a rural life," I evaded. I turned to Mr. Rockingham, who had watched our approach. "I understand you missed some of its comforts at the Rose and Crown, sir," I commented.

"Mr. Goodman did all he could," Mr. Rockingham protested. "But as I was just telling your mother, we are extremely pleased to stay at Strathamsford. I feel better already," he added gallantly.

Mama accepted this tribute with a smile, but I couldn't

leave well enough alone. "You don't yearn," I said with a sidewise glance at Mr. Strickland, "for sophisticated society or for the city's . . ." I paused to think of a word which wouldn't upset Mama.

"Pleasures," Mr. Strickland suggested.

"Pleasures?" I finished my question. I did not look at my prompter.

"Strathamsford is perfect," said Mr. Rockingham cautiously. I gather, dear Brother, that our injured guest, having witnessed my ill-temper yesterday and my disordered mind today, means to walk on eggs where I am concerned. Figuratively speaking, you understand.

"Are you ill, Elizabeth?" Mama asked, reaching out to feel my forehead.

"Why, no, Mama," I protested. "Mr. Strickland was just telling me how much he values sleep. I wonder that he doesn't avoid the city altogether, where I believe the—uh—pleasures often require late hours."

Mama adjusted her motion to grasp my arm firmly. "No wonder you had the headache yesterday," she said with alarm. "You were coming down with delirium." She turned to the others. "My daughter is always sensible when she is well," she insisted. "I beg you to forgive her."

"If Elizabeth is ill, we must be going," said Mrs. Black sympathetically. (You know, of course, that the whole story, with embellishments, will be all over the county by Friday teatime.)

Jeremy patted my arm in commiseration. "I knew you must be feeling poorly," he said earnestly. "We'll talk again soon."

(Do you suppose he means to renew his suit once I am "recovered"? I am not eager to play that scene a second time.)

My good-bys were jumbled as Mama hustled me into the house and escorted me all the way to my chamber, telling Nan that I was to be kept in bed until I am myself again.

So here I am, with empty hours stretching before me in which to rue my impetuous tongue. Why do I allow that man to unsettle me? And how will Mama entertain lofty guests, let alone cope with the estate in harvest, if she imprisons me in my chamber?

For this evening, though, I will simply luxuriate in the chance to catch up on some sleep. (As somebody or other would undoubtedly say.)

Bulletins will be forthcoming. As I hope they will be returning.

Love from
Elizabeth

Conversation revised

Jeremy Black: You were in my thoughts while I was (sniff sniff) visiting in Exeter.

Elizabeth: You wonder if I was thinking of you?

J: Yes, I do.

E: I wasn't.

J (with a great show of understanding): No, you were concerned with the fire. You are all that is sweet and good.

E: Jeremy, I think we misunderstand each other.

J: You are hesitant because I have shown the depth of my affection. But I will teach you what love is. (He reaches to embrace her.)

E (stepping back): I doubt that very seriously.

J: You'll not get another offer (sniff sniff) half as good.

E: Perhaps not. But you must find someone who thinks you the handsomest man living in England.

J: You don't believe that?

E: No, Jeremy.

J: Really? You don't?

E: I'm sorry.
J: I don't know what Mother will say.
E: Plenty, I'd guess. And to anyone who will listen.

Ah, Brother. How did a nice man like you get a shrew for a sister? I have been given time to ponder the question.

E.

Thursday, 7 October, 1813

Dearest Brother,

For two whole days I have been deliciously lazy. Please forgive my gloating to one who serves his king in a foreign war. But it is a rare treat even for me. Although I had planned to go back to work tomorrow, I think I shall take just one more day.

Nan and I have managed to head off a crisis or two by suggesting a course of action to Uncle, who proposes it to Mama.

Mama decided, for instance, Nan reported, that our more agile guest might be entertained by the harvest festival in the village. (Can you imagine our tenants enjoying themselves under the haughty eye of Mr. Strickland?) So Nan reminded Uncle that the party is likely to be boisterous, and perhaps not the most favourable impression of our village for well-bred guests. When he relayed the message to Mama I gather he included not only the word "boisterous" but also the word "drunken." Nan has heard nothing further about inviting Mr. Strickland to the harvest festival.

Dr. Harrison called on me yesterday morning—of course Mama sent for him at once—and was willing to concur with Mama's diagnosis, since I had no immediate objection. Because Mama has further decreed that my delirium may be contagious, only Nan is allowed entrance to my chamber. The day is far longer, I find, when it is not broken into its usual patterns. I struggled much of today with the ledgers—Nan smuggled them up—to no avail.

So tonight, when I expected everyone else to be abed, I slipped quietly to the library to choose a book or two for my quarantine. There, not at all surprised to see me, was Uncle.

"Ah, the invalid," he said.

I tried to look wan. "I thought perhaps a book of sermons might help me sleep," I explained.

Uncle spoke to the portrait of Great Grandmother above the globe. "The young lady believes she can bamboozle her daft old uncle."

I coughed piteously.

"Her malady has two symptoms, I think," Uncle said, still addressing Great Grandmother. "She has an overquick tongue and a lack of enthusiasm for the company of our guests."

"Well, one of them anyway," I agreed. "Uncle, Uncle, I am teasing," I admitted. "I knew from the beginning that you weren't fooled."

"Speaking of the beginning," Uncle said firmly, "explain to me, if you will, what in the world you and Mr. Strickland were talking about. What I heard sounded exceedingly strange."

"I'm sure it did," I said, laughing. "He is a challenging conversationalist. Have you ever known me to back down from a challenge?"

"Not until your current—shall we say?—illness," Uncle conceded.

"I'll be well soon," I promised. "You won't give me away?"

He turned to look me in the eye. "Did I tell your mother when your brother took you to a boxing meet?"

"No, Uncle," I said.

"Or that you hid in the oak tree last month when Jeremy Black came to call and stayed there until he was well gone?"

"No, Uncle."

"Maybe your mother and I should have a long talk."

"No, Uncle," I repeated fondly. "I'm not the only bamboozler in this family." I picked up a candle and held it close to a shelf to read the spines of the books. "What should I read tomorrow?"

"What do you find to dislike in our guests?" Uncle asked without ceremony.

"Maybe Shakespeare," I suggested. *"Much Ado About Nothing?"*

"Perhaps *The Comedy of Errors,*" Uncle proposed.

"More like *The Tempest,*" I said wryly.

"And that is why you avoid the company of our guests?" Uncle asked. "Because you do not keep your temper in their presence?"

"Oh, Uncle," I said. "One has a sweet disposition but little wit; and the other has, I believe, a keen wit but a disdainful temper." I paused to think and put my candle on the library table. "Certainly I wish I could control my temper. But Mr. Strickland is an infuriating man. He simply dares me to behave outrageously." I plunged on. "And his dismissal of Nan was indefensible. He acted as if she were lint on his jacket. A mere annoyance to be brushed to the floor."

"Mr. Strickland does not know Nan," Uncle defended.

"Exactly," I said. "He irritates me into losing my temper. And Mama is upset just when she needs calm. Think how wretched she would be if she knew why I pleaded a headache."

"Your mother seems to be holding up well under the

pressures of an unplanned houseparty," Uncle said cautiously.

"Yes, she does," I agreed. "If she is to continue to hold up well, it is best that I have as little as possible to do with either Mr. Strickland or his injured friend."

Uncle spoke again to Great Grandmother's portrait. "The young lady's mother may entertain hopes regarding the visiting gentlemen."

"'Designs,' I think, is the word, Uncle," I corrected. Then what he had said sank into my head. "You don't think so?" I asked. "We know them not at all."

Uncle tilted his head at the portrait. "Two unmarried gentlemen drop out of the sky and she insists that a mother is oblivious to the possibilities for her unpromised daughter."

"Mama has not so much as hinted at it," I said in rebuttal. "In fact, she has sent me to my bed."

"She reacted to her worry of the moment," Uncle answered. Then he dropped his serious tone. "I foresee her willingness to accept your marvelous recovery."

"You are quite mistaken, Uncle," I said haltingly. "I fear I am suffering a relapse." I grabbed several volumes and moved to the door like one with a rapidly sickening constitution.

Uncle laughed. "I'm sketching tomorrow at the abbey," he said to my back. "Perhaps you will feel well enough to accompany me?"

"Good night," I said weakly. As I started up the stairs I looked daggers at him over my shoulder. He knows the abbey is my special favourite. I suspect he decided to go on the instant, just to tease me.

Maybe I will have my relapse tomorrow night instead of tonight. If only you were here, we would plot a way.

I wonder what you would think of our guests. Mr. Rockingham appears amiable, what little I have seen of him, but he is older than his friend and does not seem the sort who would relish conspiring in one of your renowned pranks. You might, however, make a cohort of Mr. Strickland, at least until he showed you the arrogance behind the twinkle in his eye. You would find a way to puncture his self-importance, I'm sure.

Neither have I been able to talk all this over with Nan. She has been—did I tell you?—preoccupied of late, so we have not discussed the current situation as we used to do. She is invaluable help as always, but if we don't need her, she spends her time in her chamber "writing letters" or "keeping her journal." And you could guess she is more disorganised than ever. I haven't decided what to make of it, and of course it must seem the merest problem to you. But I miss her.

I have worked out how to go with Uncle tomorrow. Just after dawn I will take my mare to the copse beyond the sheep pasture. Uncle will think it a rare joke if I join him on the way. And Cook always packs enough luncheon for four. I can take the footstool cover I am decorating with needlepoint for Mama's Christmas. Progress is very slow.

If I weren't supposed to be ill, I would call on Sarah Brown and her new son. I seem to be trapped in my own deception. Wouldn't it be heartening if I learned from my misdeeds?

Yes, you may send me a lecture. If only you will write to

Your loving sister,
Elizabeth

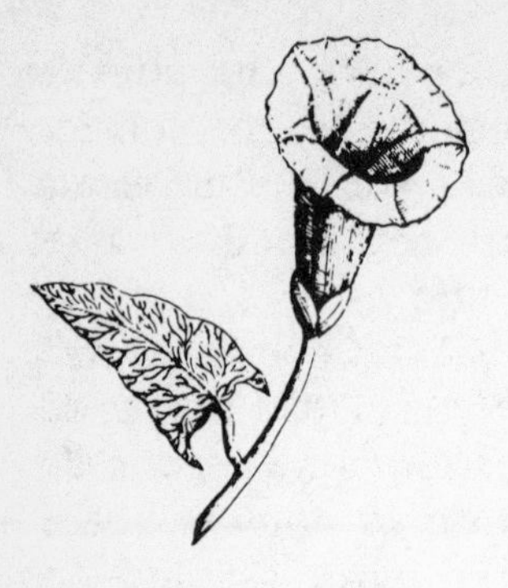

Friday, 8 October, 1813

Dearest Brother,

Why don't we hear from you? I tell myself that it is the fault of transatlantic winds and not of the correspondent, but still I am impatient. The ten days since your last letter seem like as many weeks. But of course you need not write another line, if only you will come safely home.

Last night's scheme, as you will have imagined, fell sadly awry. It began well enough. I rose before sun-up, left a note for Nan, and made an impromptu breakfast of bread and cheese on my way to the stables. Only Jem saw me tacking up Lilac, and I swore him to secrecy.

To be out of doors after two days inside was indescribably invigorating. (Maybe I am truly a farmer at heart!) It was a morning out of a fairy tale: low over the fields hung wisps of fog, to which the rising sun gave a golden glow. As I waited for Uncle I had the ridiculous feeling that a white knight would ride out of the forest as the last of the mist was conquered by the sun. So, when I heard a horseman approaching, I called out merrily.

"Uncle, rescue a maiden in distress!" Dramatically I raised the back of my hand to my forehead. "Be the knight in shining armour who whisks me off to the abbey . . ." My words trailed off as I realised to my consternation that the rider was not our Uncle but the sardonic Mr. Strickland. (The Fates can be swift: call yourself a maiden in distress in jest and, as soon as the words are uttered, they make you one in truth.)

"My shining armour is being polished, Miss Carlisle," said Mr. Strickland without smiling. "But I'd be honoured to whisk you off to the abbey. Which abbey is your wish?"

"Forgive me, sir," I said, attempting to keep my voice steady. "I mistook you for someone else."

"You're not delirious, then?" he asked. He dismounted and looked at me keenly.

"If I confess to delirium, will you forget my foolishness?" I looked him in the eye.

"I didn't think so," he said. He finally averted his gaze. "You seem perfectly healthy to me."

Contrary to an alteration of fact to make a smooth surface, which Mama has always insisted forms the basis of happy contact between the sexes, Mr. Strickland seems to prefer his truth unvarnished. He interrupted my musing.

"Is there really an abbey?" he asked.

"Indeed, yes, sir," I answered. "My uncle's primary occupation is painting in watercolours. He sketches today at Greenfield Abbey and I hope to accompany him."

Mr. Strickland did not appear to notice that my response was an unadorned statement of fact. "The autumn landscape in the upper hall. Did your uncle paint that?" he asked. He thought for a moment. "And the still life with roses in the library?"

His obvious and observant interest served to ease my irritation with him. "Yes, he did both," I answered more civilly. "My own favourite is one of the abbey after leaf-fall but before snow." He gave me a questioning look. "It hangs in the upstairs sitting room," I added.

"I will look for it," he said. "Does your uncle exhibit his work?"

Surprised, I said quickly, "Why, no. He simply paints a little."

"He paints much more than a little, my dear," Mr. Strickland contradicted me. "Unless you also consider that Thomas Gainsborough also painted a little."

"Mr. Gainsborough executed portraits in oils, sir," I objected. "Of course he painted more than a little."

"If every artist executed portraits in oils, the history of art would be monotonous," he pontificated. "Do you not agree?"

"Perhaps," I said, withholding judgement.

(Do you think of Uncle as an artist, Brother? I confess I have not.)

"It's difficult to give proper appreciation to what is overly familiar," Mr. Strickland said condescendingly.

My irritation returned with accumulated interest. "My uncle is most fondly regarded by all who know him," I said indignantly. "And his sketches greatly valued by everyone fortunate enough to possess one." My temper, running away with me yet again, was still racing out of control. "What are you doing up so early anyway?" I demanded petulantly. "You told me you guard your rest jealously."

"I couldn't sleep in all this country quiet," he said with a straight face. "We Londoners need to hear hoofbeats on the cobblestones."

I greeted that remark with the silence it deserved (no doubt he had caught up on his sleeping during my absence) and Mr. Strickland again looked at me intently. "You are not in the ordinary way of young women," he said. "What do your friends call you?"

"My friends, sir, do not need to ask," I answered, glad that those friends could not hear my insolence. (Perhaps I suffer from delirium after all. Certainly I have never before been so sullen. Do you suppose Mr. Strickland carries the germ with him?)

Just then this maiden in distress was rescued in truth:

Uncle, his horse laden with painting paraphernalia and a luncheon basket, came down the lane. When he saw Mr. Strickland and me, he jerked Sailor to a halt.

"Lily!" he exclaimed. (Honestly, Brother. Can you remember the last time anyone called me that?) "You are here with Mr. Strickland?"

"I was waiting for you, Uncle," I said quickly. "To go with you to the abbey." Out of the corner of my eye I could see Mr. Strickland taking mental note of my childhood nickname.

"I was giving my horse an early run, sir," Mr. Strickland explained. "Miss Carlisle had reached the copse before me and hailed me, expecting the rider to be you." He flickered his right eyebrow at me as Uncle looked from one of us to the other.

"It isn't a rendez-vous, then?" he asked.

"You know it is not," I said at once.

"Perhaps next time," said Mr. Strickland wickedly.

"Oh," said Uncle. There was a pause during which I glared at Mr. Strickland. "So you've decided to come with me after all," Uncle continued. He looked again from me to our guest. "Mr. Strickland has deduced that you are not in fact gravely ill?" he asked.

"He has," I said grimly.

"And does he know the reason for your deception?" Uncle continued.

"No, he does not," Mr. Strickland said. "He was just about to ask."

I transferred my glare to Uncle. "I need a rest from my social obligations," I said haughtily.

Mr. Strickland laughed, and I am sorry to tell you that Uncle joined him. "Would you care to accompany us to Greenfield Abbey, sir?" Uncle invited my tormentor. "The trip is a pleasant one and the ruin is charming."

"I promised to eat breakfast with Dan Rockingham," Mr.

Strickland said regretfully. "I wish I could, sir. It would be a privilege to watch you draw."

Uncle was startled. "You know my work?"

"Two paintings I noticed on my own, and your niece has told me of another," he explained. "You are gifted."

Uncle smiled. "I thank you, sir. I please an undiscriminating audience."

"And would delight the most discriminating," Mr. Strickland insisted. "May I see more of your collection?"

"Certainly, sir," Uncle agreed happily. "Perhaps tomorrow after luncheon? In the morning I must continue what I begin today."

"I look forward to it," Mr. Strickland said. He looked at me out of the corner of his eye. "Maybe Miss Carlisle will join us to add a feminine viewpoint."

"I'm sorry," I said demurely. "Mama may not be able to spare me tomorrow afternoon."

"Or perhaps you will need to rest," Mr. Strickland suggested, trying not to smile.

"Oh, I'm sure my niece should consult the doctor before she attempts anything as exhausting as viewing my little pictures," Uncle said, all concern.

My temper flared and I would have lashed out at both of them, but Uncle cut me off.

"Come now, Liza, don't be angry," he said conciliatingly. "We're only teasing." I frowned at him. "Don't you think it's time for you to recover from whatever?" he asked. "Let's go back early with a story for your mother."

"Perhaps, Uncle," I said, overmindful of the man who was listening. Truth to tell, my chamber was losing its appeal—familiarity breeds contempt?—and our house is large enough to avoid Mr. Strickland without hiding out.

"To the abbey?" Uncle asked to change the subject.

"Maybe you will invite me another day," Mr. Strickland said.

"It would be our pleasure," Uncle answered warmly.

"Indeed, sir," I echoed without expression. I turned away to walk over to Lilac.

Suddenly Mr. Strickland was beside me and I had a chance to say under my breath, "No one has called me Lily for a dozen years. Uncle was merely surprised."

"No matter," said Mr. Strickland as he gave me a leg up onto Lilac's back. "It will serve." He threw me a lopsided smile and I was grateful for my immunity to the charm he can display if he chooses.

He disappeared toward Strathamsford and Uncle and I continued our largely silent ride to Greenfield Abbey.

As we tethered our horses there, Uncle looked at me thoughtfully. "You seem always to be at cross-purposes with our guest."

I did not need to ask which guest he meant. "He has the sensitivity of a sword," I said.

"His wit is sharp too," Uncle commented.

"Yes," I agreed. "He fancies it cuts deep." I picked up my letter box, ignoring once again my poor needlepoint, and started toward the inner cloister. Tiring of repartee, I said simply, "I cannot like him."

"Oh," Uncle said; he seemed content to leave it at that.

Thus we are spending the day at the abbey. There is autumn in the leaves, and I have eaten so many blackberries that my interest in luncheon is virtually nonexistent, as you can tell from the smears on this letter.

I wish I could send blackberries and cream. Surely you will be home long before next year's crop. Yours will be picked by

Elizabeth

Conversation revised

Mr. Strickland: You seem perfectly healthy to me.
Elizabeth: Truly, I think the early morning air has a restor-

ative effect. (Pause.) But, sir, I thought that morning air did not agree with you.

Mr. S: It agrees with my horse, ma'am, so occasionally I risk its dangers.

E: Voyageur looks a prime goer. But his name is a mouthful.

Mr. S: Because I know him well, I call him Joe. (Pats horse's neck.) What are you called by those who know you well, Miss Carlisle?

E: My given name is Elizabeth, sir.

Uncle (approaching on horseback): Lily? You are here with Mr. Strickland. Do I intrude?

Mr. S: No, sir. I believe it is I who acts the intruder.

U: Nonsense. Will you go with us to Greenfield Abbey? I sketch there today.

Mr. S: You draw, sir?

U: A little, yes.

E: My uncle is overmodest.

Mr. S: You painted the still life in the dining room? The lily has long been my favourite flower.

U: Yes. My hapless sister feels constrained to cover her walls with my swashes.

Mr. S: I'd say instead that she is fortunate to have a resident artist. (Under his breath) Not to mention a resident Lily.

E: Have you heard, sir? We have a new strain of lily, one which has thorns.

Mr. S: I shall count on your goodness, Miss Carlisle, to help me pull the stickers from my finger.

Do you believe it, Brother? Not only did I revise a conversation toward Mama's standards, but I failed to get the last word.

Do you suppose he really calls his horse Joe?

E.

Saturday, 9 October, 1813

Dearest Brother,

I am now officially declared recovered from the delirium. Mama did not discover my absence yesterday, but when she came to my chamber after tea, she decided that I looked so improved I might join the company for the evening.

"If you won't get overtired, dear," she said. "I recommend a tray here, but after supper you may come down." Her tone became confidential. "I am eager for you to become better acquainted with our visitors. I find them quite charming."

"And unmarried," I commented.

"You mustn't hold their bachelorhood against them," Mama protested. "It isn't their fault." (What she means, dear Brother, is that they have not yet encountered a mother with her own innocent guile.)

"I shan't," I said. "But neither shall I polish my hope chest."

"I ask only that you be open-minded," Mama said. (What she means is empty-headed.)

"Yes, Mama," I agreed obediently. And after supper Nan

ne gown Mama had suggested and arranged

et your own hair ribbon," I reminded Nan as
a strip of grosgrain through my curls.
not going downstairs," she protested.
rse you are," I stated firmly. "We are used to enjoying your company after supper. And I, for one, refuse to exchange it for that of our arrogant guest."

"He will be more arrogant if I am present, you know he will," she insisted.

"Let him try," I threatened. "Just let him try."

"Would it not be easier on your mother if I stayed upstairs?" Nan made a final plea. "She has drunk little more than wine with dinner since the fire, and I would not be the cause . . ." She let her words trail off.

"Please, Nan," I coaxed. "You can trust me not to upset Mama. No more delirium, I promise." I opened the drawer to my dressing table. "Now, your hair ribbon: ivory or blue?"

So together we went downstairs. And the evening, in truth, was much more pleasant than I expected. When we entered the drawing room, the others were already assembled. I led Nan over to Mr. Rockingham, who sat in the big chair by the fire, his leg on a footstool.

"Good evening, sir," I said. "How nice to see you looking so well. You remember my friend Nan Andrews?"

"Of course," answered Mr. Rockingham graciously. "I'm glad you both could join us." He included Nan in his smile before he turned to me. "And that you, too, are feeling better."

"Good evening, Miss Carlisle, Miss Andrews," interrupted Mr. Strickland. He raised one eyebrow at his friend. "Your ailments were somewhat dissimilar," he commented drily.

Mama gave a girlish giggle. "Of course, sir," she said.

"A lady has a more delicate nature. But I trust Elizabeth is strong enough to sit with us for a few minutes."

"One would hardly guess your daughter has been ill," Mr. Strickland said with a glance at me, "she looks so well."

"Yes, doesn't she?" Mama said, beaming.

Uncle tried to rescue me for the second time yesterday. "This morning I sketched at the abbey, Liza," he said in all truth. "I think this time to paint it from the eastern view."

"You must see his drawings, Miss Carlisle," urged Mr. Rockingham. "The abbey looks most picturesque."

I nodded. "The abbey is one of the loveliest spots in the county," I agreed. "I visit it often."

"Oh?" asked Mr. Strickland wickedly.

Nan tried almost successfully to hide a smile and I glared at Mr. Strickland as I spoke to his friend. "Perhaps when you are able to make a short trip, we can take you there."

Mama had been sorting through her sewing bag for the thread she wanted for her petit point. "I could wish that Liza was artistic," she said thoughtfully. "But she is a gifted musician."

Oh, Brother, you know how I hate it when she trots out my modest accomplishments. Over my blush, Mr. Rockingham said politely, "I'm very fond of music. Will you play for us?"

"I've been ill, as you know, sir," I said apologetically, "and have not practised." Mr. Strickland coughed. "Maybe we could . . ." I paused while my mind raced over possibilities, "play whist?"

"Yes, you might play cards," Mama agreed. "You young people. Nan, would you get the table, please?"

Mr. Strickland got up to take the table from her and I thought perhaps I had misjudged him. Then he spoke and I knew I had not. "You are perceptive to count Dan

Rockingham among the young at heart, ma'am,'' he said to Mama. Then he looked to Uncle. ''Will you be my partner, sir?'' he asked.

Do you see, Brother? Nan doesn't exist. It never occurred to him that Mama expected her to hold the fourth hand. I bit my tongue to keep from saying something sharp, and Uncle answered his question.

''Liza is my usual opposite, Mr. Strickland,'' he said. ''Since she has been ill, perhaps she would find it easier to play with a familiar partner.''

''Of course,'' said Mr. Strickland smoothly. ''We can switch around once Miss Carlisle has recovered the bloom of health.'' (You can guess, Brother, which word received his emphasis.) Mr. Strickland should not hold his breath. Or maybe he should. (You can see how ill-tempered I become with advanced years.)

So Nan slipped away, Mama worked her petit point, and the rest of us played whist for a long evening. It gives me enormous pleasure to report that Uncle and I trounced our visitors. When they asked for the stakes so as to figure their debt, we assured them that shillings never cross our card table, which for some reason made the victory even sweeter.

When I reached my chamber it was late; and I apologised earnestly to Nan for Mr. Strickland's casual assumption that she would not play cards.

''Nonsense, Liza,'' she said. ''I was relieved not to play, truly I was. I used the time to finish several things.'' Then she hurried to bed.

Now I ask you, Brother: is this the candid Nan you remember? Maybe Mama knows what is wrong.

But Mama won't arise for hours yet and I have much to do before then.

So why, I wonder, do I waste time rewriting conversations?

Conversation revised

Mr. Rockingham: I'm glad you too are feeling better, Miss Carlisle.

Mr. Strickland: Your ailments were greatly dissimilar.

Mama: A lady has a more delicate nature. But I trust Elizabeth is strong enough to sit at the spinet.

Mr. S: Your accomplishments are delicate too, Miss Carlisle?

E: In truth, sir, I play cards better than the pianoforte. May I give you a lesson?

Mr. S: Surely you jest. I would no more expect to learn cards from you than from your maid.

E: She could teach you as well as I, sir.

Mr. S: No doubt, ma'am.

E: Never underestimate the enemy, Mr. Strickland. Will you deal?

To work!

Love from
Elizabeth

Monday, 11 October, 1813

Dearest Brother,

Your letters from Strathamsford may be shorter now that I have stopped playing truant and begun playing hostess. Or they may be even longer, if I try to chronicle all our bustling about. I wish only that your activities were so innocuous.

After Nan and I ate breakfast in the kitchen yesterday morning, she left for the south farm. I asked her to tell Jane Ludlow that I would try to stop by before luncheon to admire the repairs to the cottage and to deliver Nan's and my small gift to young Thomas.

Then I stayed on in the kitchen to plan our menus through the next week. Mama, as you might guess, has been requesting meals a good deal more elaborate than we are accustomed to, and the larder must be replenished. Cook and I at length agreed on a series of meals with which we hope to satisfy both the staff and our guests as well as Mama. We prepared a sizeable list for the shops in the village and I promised to take the carriage to town this afternoon. I was intending to find Sally to check for needs in her domain, when Mama called to me from the breakfast room.

"Good morning, Mama," I answered, going in to speak with her.

"Come sit with me while I finish my coffee," she invited. "How are you feeling today?"

"Very well, thank you," I answered. "And the Holland bulbs. Has Jem finished digging them up?"

"Oh yes, dear," Mama said. "Since repairs are complete at the south farm, he has time for gardening."

Her mentioning the south farm reminded me. "I expect to ride over to the Ludlows' in an hour or so to see the new roof," I said. "Why don't you come with me?"

"I couldn't possibly," Mama insisted. "We do have guests, you know, and I have promised Mr. Rockingham my special Yorkshire pudding."

"For tonight, Mama?" I asked. "Did you mention it to Cook? We'll have to rearrange our menus."

"Surely that's no problem, Liza." Mama softened her rebuttal with a smile. "He's so looking forward to it."

"Of course it isn't," I agreed. "We all look forward to your special Yorkshire pudding." (If I could, Brother, I would send a portion with this letter—my mouth is watering already.) I made a mental note to confer with Cook.

"I've been wanting to talk to you," Mama and I both started in unison.

"Nan," I said.

"Yes, Nan," Mama answered. "Do you think she's well?"

"I've been worrying about her too," I admitted. "Yes, I believe whatever is wrong is not with her health. She seems preoccupied."

"That's what it is," Mama concurred. "Her mind is somewhere else." She thought a moment. "Does she not talk to you?"

"She talks to me," I said. "But she no longer confides in me. And I don't wish to pry."

"Maybe she's in love," Mama suggested.

"I had considered that explanation," I conceded. "But—"

Mama interrupted me. "If that's the answer, I wonder who he is?" Her eyes took on added fire. "You don't suppose she's hoping to attach Jeremy Black!"

"No, Mama," I said. I couldn't suppress a giggle.

"Don't laugh, Liza," Mama commanded. "I saw her watch the two of you Tuesday when you took Rascal to the barn."

"Mama, I can assure you Nan does not yearn for Jeremy Black," I said with conviction, and my tone apparently satisfied her.

"I'm glad," she said.

"So am I," I agreed, although I would wager our reasons were different.

Mama's imagination continued to work overtime. "Not one of our guests? Do you think?"

"Definitely not," I dissented. "We're getting carried away, Mama," I declared. "The reason for her preoccupation is no doubt far afield from our guesses."

"I'm sure you're right," Mama sighed. "But it disturbs me. She is so quiet now."

"But she is, of course, shy around our guests," I said. "All the more reason to disbelieve any partiality."

"And you, Liza?" she asked carefully. "Could you like Mr. Strickland? Or even Mr. Rockingham? He's too old for you but—"

"I think not, Mama," I said. "Do you have a letter ready for my brother? I'm going to the village this afternoon and I could post it for you." (Surely you do not mind being used in an attempt to deflect Mama from consideration of my spinsterhood.)

"I knew there was something I needed to do," Mama said, putting her napkin on the table and pushing back her chair. "Yes, please see me before you go to the village." And she rushed from the breakfast room.

Then, of course, I got caught up in a myriad of household tangles—yes, I remembered to tell Cook about the

Yorkshire pudding—and by the time I was ready to leave for the south farm it was so nearly time for luncheon that I decided to combine the visit with my trip to the village in the afternoon. Besides, when I go in the carriage, Rascal is willing to be left behind: his huge size coupled with his bounding energy frightens the children.

It was going on three o'clock when I finally arrived at the south farm; Nan was helping her sister sew attic curtains to replace the ones lost in the fire. Jane walked around the outside of the cottage with me, so that I could admire the new roof from every angle. She is very proud of it. I myself think it will look better once the shingles have weathered to be less eye-catching, but I said all that was appropriate.

Thomas was playing in a heap of fallen leaves near the road when we finished our tour, and I called him over to the carriage. Did I tell you that he lost his coverlet in the fire? He has been desolate, Nan reported to me, so she and I (while I was supposedly suffering from the delirium) quilted a new one for him. Thomas thanked us sweetly with only a little prodding from his mother when Nan and I presented him with the new blanket. But it was obvious he thought our gift a poor substitute.

"It's such a lovely blue," Jane prompted her son. Thomas looked suspicious. "You're very kind," she said to me. "I'm sure he will prize it highly by nightfall."

"I'm sorry he doesn't like it more right now," I said with a grimace. "But truly, Nan did most of the work." I turned to Nan. "Will you ride back with me?" I asked. "It must be late and Mama is making Yorkshire pudding."

"I'll stay a little longer, if you don't mind," Nan said. She and Jane exchanged glances. "Jane and I hope to hang the curtains this afternoon."

"Of course you should stay," I agreed. "Until dinner, then." Nan smiled gratefully and Jane thanked me for my visit.

"The cottage looks better than before," I said honestly. "You've done a fine job."

Jane beamed. "Come again soon, Liza." She spotted the coverlet where Thomas had left it on the doorsill. "And thank-you."

"I will," I promised, and climbed into the carriage. I waved at Thomas, who waved shyly back. I'll come back very soon, I continued to myself, to see if Jane knows what is upsetting Nan. I'll let you know, Brother.

Later.

Actually, it's now Tuesday afternoon. My letters are reaching an absurd length. I hope you don't try to save them. Soon you will have no space left in your baggage for clean linen.

Thanks to Rascal, I returned to the south farm even sooner than I expected to. Your aptly named animal appeared at the door of my chamber this morning dragging behind him the coverlet Nan and I had presented to Thomas Ludlow yesterday afternoon. Except that now the colour Jane had praised was dulled by the dirt and leaves the quilt had picked up on its journey back.

"Oh, Rascal!" Nan and I cried out as one. I gathered up the poor coverlet and ran downstairs to shake it out at the kitchen door. Then Nan washed it out and spread it before the kitchen fire to dry. All the while we explained to your dog that we meant for Thomas to keep the quilt for his own.

When the coverlet was dry, I rode Lilac to the south farm, so that Rascal would come with me and see me give it to Thomas with his own eyes.

At the Ludlows' cottage, Thomas and Missy were having an early supper. Rascal was overjoyed. Food! Missy shrank into her high chair. Thomas screwed up his face as if he were going to cry until I held Rascal's collar with one hand and held out the coverlet to Thomas with the other. And guess what? Now that the quilt is bedraggled, Thomas is enchanted with it.

He has also decided that your beloved animal is boy's best friend. He was about to slip Rascal a bun from his supper, when I asked him not to feed the dog at the table. So Thomas jumped down with the bun and ran out the back door calling, "Wasco. Here, Wasco." Rascal knew whom he meant.

When I finally pulled the dog away, Thomas watched us until we were out of sight, clasping the coverlet to his heart with both hands. There must be a moral to this story somewhere.

The moral is not, I've found, write letters and ye shall receive. It is far too long since we had word of you. I can only assume that no news is good news. But good news would be better. You know where to send it.

But now I suppose I must continue with my story. Perhaps you have guessed that what comes next I would just as soon forget. If only you were here, maybe I could laugh—at my antagonist, if not at myself.

Rascal, Lilac, and I were taking the road home at an easy gait, since Rascal was full of buns and I was marvelling at the incident of the coverlet, when all three of us realised that a horseman approached from Strathamsford. It was, of course, my nemesis, Mr. Strickland.

"Miss Carlisle," he said as he came abreast and pulled up Voyageur.

There was nothing I could do but stop as well. "Mr. Strickland," I replied. Rascal flopped down at the side of the road.

"It's a beautiful afternoon," he said. "The morning looked so threatening that I postponed my ride." I smiled in agreement. "Shall we go together?" he asked. "Or are you on your way home?"

"Yes, I am," I answered. "I've just made a quick call at our south farm."

"No one could guess that there had been a fire," Mr. Strickland commented. "I've ridden by almost daily as repairs progressed."

"I hope Mr. Rockingham's injury is soon as unnoticeable," I said. "He seems better each day, too."

"Though perhaps we would not wish his leg as shiny new as the cottage roof," Mr. Strickland suggested. "There is much to be said in favour of a few years experience."

"Both for roofs and for legs, you mean?" I laughed. "I agree."

He laughed too. "May I ride back with you?" he asked. Without waiting for my answer, he turned his horse so that we headed in the same direction. "Why is it," he went on, "that although you and I are staying in the same house, we never talk except out of doors and out of company?"

"That's not true," I protested. "I distinctly remember asking you at luncheon to pass the plum preserve."

Mr. Strickland made a dismissing gesture with the hand that held his reins, and Voyageur obediently began to walk toward Strathamsford. "Exactly," he said. I touched Lilac with my heel and tsked for Rascal. "Your mother's management of mealtime conversation is light but firm," he continued as all of us moved slowly up the road.

"Mama believes that social interchange should not cut too deep," I defended. "Do you not concur?"

"To be superficial is often to be tedious," he proclaimed.

"You find my mother tedious, sir?" I challenged.

"Don't fly up at me, Miss Carlisle," Mr. Strickland ordered. "I had merely wished to compliment you on your card sense. You play well."

"I had a good teacher," I said briefly, still annoyed with him.

"Oh?" he asked.

"My brother declared that he would not allow me to disgrace our family at the whist table," I grudgingly explained. "But I believe he simply wanted competent competition." (Am I right, Brother dear?)

"You miss him, don't you?" Mr. Strickland asked.

"Oh, yes, I do," I said emphatically. I chuckled in spite of myself imagining your reaction to the coverlet story.

"Do you always laugh about missing someone?" he asked curiously.

"Please excuse me," I beseeched him. "It's just that his beloved Rascal has gotten into mischief yet again." And I found myself telling Mr. Strickland the whole of the tale about young Thomas and his quilt.

"Rascal watches out for you," my companion observed through his laughter. Our horses were walking so slowly as to be almost at a standstill.

"I suppose he does," I said. "But I wish he would concede that I am capable of watching out for myself."

"Is that why you ride alone?" Mr. Strickland asked. "If you have no groom to spare, shouldn't your maid accompany you?"

I took a deep breath in hope of defusing my rising anger. "Stratham is my backyard, sir," I said expressionlessly. "I have nothing to fear and no one to impress."

He pulled Voyageur to a stop. "Has anyone ever told you that you take offense very easily?" he asked.

"I 'take offense,' as you put it, at arrogance," I retorted. "Your disdain for those you consider beneath you infuriates me." I rode on ahead of him.

"Come back here!" Mr. Strickland demanded. While I resisted obedience to his imperative tone, I did halt Lilac so that he could catch me. "What do you mean, 'arrogance'?" he asked in a more normal voice. "I assume you consider that I malign Nan Andrews." I nodded. "She is your maid, is she not?" he continued. "Surely it is her place to serve you. Women who employ maids do not usually gallivant by themselves around the countryside."

"You treat Mr. Rockingham as a friend," I answered. "Yet he is in service to you as your man of business."

"And serves me very well," Mr. Strickland declared. "But he is educated, a professional man. He is no more a member of the servant class than a doctor is."

I was furious. Servant class, indeed. "Our conversation is tedious and our servants shirk their duties," I reviewed for him. "Is there anything you wish to tell me about any other members of our household?"

"Come down from the boughs, my dear," the man soothed. "You become incensed when I least expect it. I meant no insult to your cherished maid."

I glared at him and said nothing.

"Truce?" Mr. Strickland asked. "I apologise for any offense against you and yours." He gave me a smile which I'm sure some would rate irresistible.

In my irritation I found it merely charming. But the man is our guest. "Truce," I said.

"Besides," he added wickedly, "there is indeed something else I would like to tell you about another member of your household. It concerns your uncle."

"Tell me later," I said. I kicked Lilac into a canter and we raced toward Strathamsford with Rascal trying unsuccessfully to keep pace. I don't know how Mr. Strickland and Voyageur continued their ride; I did not look back.

It's now almost time for dinner and I have regained my composure sufficiently to finish up this voluminous text. Truly, life at Strathamsford is not always so fractious.

In fact, we seem to have fallen into a comfortable domestic routine, which apparently suits our guests as well as those who live at Strathamsford. As Mr. Strickland commented, I see very little of the visitors. He joins Mr. Rockingham in Papa's study for breakfast, after which I think he usually rides. I spend the morning with orders and bills, household and tenants' problems, and do not see either man until luncheon, which we take on the terrace since the days have remained pleasant.

After luncheon I escape to the drawing room to practise the spinet or walk to the village or ride. Mama makes and receives calls as usual. The guests join Uncle in his studio until midafternoon—Mr. Rockingham is learning to walk with the aid of crutches. Then while Mr. Rockingham rests, Uncle drops by the Rose and Crown and Mr. Strickland disappears into the library to do whatever such a gentleman does in a library. Today, as you know already, he did not—alas—stay in the library.

We are together, of course, at dinner, but Mr. Strickland was right: Mama sees to it that the conversation is both unbroken and general. And last evening Dr. Harrison stopped by to examine the patient, so we were spared even a mention of cards or music.

Now I must dress for dinner. Do you wish a report of tonight's discourse?

Conversation revised

Mr. Strickland: Why is it that you and I never talk except out of doors and out of company?

Elizabeth: Perhaps one of us is avoiding the other, sir.

Mr. S: I'm sure *I* would not.

E: Exactly.

Mr. S: You begrudge me a few moments of nontedious conversation, ma'am?

E: No more than you, sir, begrudge Nan Andrews the right to stay at home if she chooses.

Mr. S: The examples are somewhat different, you must admit.

E: Yes, no doubt your idea of similar examples is Nan and Rascal. Both should follow me around and do as they're told.

Mr. S: Surely your maid does not steal coverlets from small boys?
E: This, sir, is a tedious conversation.
Mr. S (flashing brilliant smile): Truce?
E: Has any woman yet refused you?
Mr. S: No.
E: Then this afternoon is memorable for you. Good day, sir.

Such an ill-tempered sister you have. If only I could believe that by imagining a crosspatch conversation on letter paper, I will speak with unfailing courtesy in company.

I do miss you!

Love from
Elizabeth

P.S. Your dog, you will be pleased to hear, is becoming beloved by sharp-tongued sisters as well as small boys. While Rascal and I were returning the coverlet to the south farm, Jeremy called at Strathamsford to see me, and I *missed* him.

P.P.S. I just realised that I forgot to ask Jane Ludlow if she knows what is bothering Nan. I hope I am not to combine Nan's scatterbrains with my ill-temper. A pretty picture indeed of

E.

Wednesday, 13 October, 1813

Dearest Brother,

For what I suspect (and trust) is the first time, you may rejoice that you are not at home. Guess who has appeared with three trunks and five bandboxes? Aunt Charlotte and Cousin Clarissa! Our attraction is not hard to deduce. The only puzzle is how they found out.

Nan and I were in the hothouse arranging centerpieces for dinner when their carriage rolled up to the front door Tuesday afternoon. So I had no inkling of their arrival until I heard a barrage of unfinished sentences from the hall.

"Really we tried to get away sooner but dear Clarissa is so popular that . . . If we had but known you had other guests, we would never . . . Elizabeth looks hale and . . . I've always liked her in that blue gown with . . ." I'm sure I need not continue for your benefit; you can imagine Aunt Charlotte's conversation all too well. One must still take Father's sister with a whole spoonful of salt.

Cousin Clarissa, too, is as frippish as ever. Also as pretty as ever. She arranges her hair in a new way, which I suppose is all the rage in London: piled carelessly on top of her head with curls artfully escaping at regular intervals. And she did not bring her maid. I wonder if Nan must learn to fix it. But excuse my boring a brother with feminine folderol.

You would have been amazed as well as amused by the inquisition at dinner. Aunt Charlotte can actually finish a sentence when she is digging for information! Sentence after sentence, in fact. She assumed control of the conversation, and our guests must have felt under questioning by the chief constable. Uncle and I tried to steer the talk to more general subjects, but even Mama herself managed to work in an occasional query.

I am ashamed to admit that I was as fascinated by the gentlemen's answers as their questioners were. (Clarissa merely seemed stunned by the size of the ruby in Mr. Strickland's cravat.) Aunt Charlotte was able to elicit that Mr. Rockingham is a clergyman's son, educated by the county squire to serve as his man of business. The squire, of course, was Mr. Strickland's father; our haughty guest inherited the accountant along with the estates at his father's death some years ago.

Mr. Strickland revealed as little as he could without being rude, but we learned that he spent a number of years, before his father died, with the East India Company. Although he claims only a superficial knowledge of silks—you can hear Cousin Clarissa's excited inquiries about dress goods—he managed trade in several provinces in both spices and tea, and soon came to specialise, he confessed with prompting from Mr. Rockingham, in the acquisition of gems, which, dear Brother, explains the eye-popping contents of his jewel case. (Have I mentioned his stickpins? I had begun to suspect they were paste.)

As soon as dinner was over, Cousin Clarissa pleaded exhaustion, announced it had been far too long since she and I had a cozy chat, and dragged me off to the upstairs sitting room almost before Nan could confer with me about Aunt Charlotte's request for breakfast trays. With the sitting room door closed behind us, Clarissa plopped down on the settee and tucked her feet up under her skirt. "So tell me at once, Lizzy, how you are getting on," she said confidentially. "Such a stroke of luck, your having a fire as they passed by. I vow I was green with envy. Which one do you like?"

An apt pupil at the maternal knee, our Clarissa. Which unkind thought and my less than straightforward reply were prompted by my hearty dislike of being called Lizzy.

"We get on famously," I told her. "Yes, the fire was incredibly fortunate." Irony alas is lost on Cousin Clarissa. So foolishly I led her on. "I haven't decided yet which of the gentlemen to attach," I said in apparent deliberation. "What do you think?"

Clarissa jumped to the bait. "Each is perfectly presentable," she said. She paused while I wondered how she would stake out the richer man for herself; she did not fail me. "Of course Mr. Rockingham is a trifle old for me," she added.

"Do you think so?" I asked. "I guess his age at not much over forty. He is hardly tottering on the brink of senility."

Clarissa brushed my comments aside. "He's probably fine for you. But I get on better with men closer to my own age." She smiled. "Mama says it's my modern outlook."

"So you would choose Mr. Strickland for yourself," I said, remembering nastily that none of the younger men who find Cousin Clarissa so appealing has yet come up to scratch.

"Oh, yes, Cousin Liza," she said excitedly. "I find him most charming. And just think of the jewels his wife will have." She hesitated one last time. "You're sure that your affections are not engaged there?" she asked.

"No, Clarissa, they most assuredly are not," I reiterated firmly and honestly.

"Wonderful. Then it's settled," she bubbled. "What shall I wear tomorrow?"

Remorse struck, as it usually does, too late to be of use.

I had realised that I should not throw even a calculating lamb to that arrogant wolf—he will, I'm sure, brush her off more politely perhaps but just as effectively as he brushed off Nan—when Mama bustled into the room.

"Here you are, girls," she chattered. "Catching up on secrets, are you?" She plumped a pillow and straightened a chair. "Your mother is asking for you, Clarissa," she continued. "She hopes you will direct the unpacking."

"She has the green chamber, does she not?" Clarissa asked. "I am not afraid to unpack when we come to Strathamsford," she giggled, "because I know that if Alice neglected to put in long gloves or a sash, I can always borrow from Lizzy." With that comforting thought, she was gone.

Mama lost no time with idle chitchat. "What did she say, Liza?" she asked immediately. "Did she confess that they are here because of our other guests?"

"She wished to know which man I have chosen," I said drily.

"What did you answer?" Mama sounded truly interested.

"I teased her by saying I had not decided, so she has picked Mr. Strickland," I reported.

"Do you mind?" Mama asked with concern. "Mr. Rockingham is much the nicer, I think."

"Of course I don't mind, Mama," I said forcefully. "These men remain with us only because of an accident. They are not here to seek wives."

Mama heard only the first part of my speech. "It is an ill wind that bloweth no man to good," she quoted.

"Mama!" I pleaded. "If we set caps for these men, we impose on their goodwill and make fools of ourselves. And we risk chasing them away before Mr. Rockingham can travel without further injury."

Mama continued as if I had not spoken. "Nan must find time to make up your new gold gown," she announced. "Did you see how many trunks they brought?"

Honestly, Brother, I felt like crying. One can only hope that our visitors will see, as you would, the absurdities in the situation.

Conversation revised

Clarissa: Which one have you picked?
Elizabeth: You consider them ripe?
C: Mr. Rockingham is perhaps overripe. A little greenness suits me better.
E: You may find Mr. Strickland too tart for your taste.
C: No doubt I can sweeten him up.
Mama: If the plates are gold, Clarissa will not even notice the taste.
E: I find I have lost my appetite for all but bread and milk.

Such nonsense! Of course there has been no time to rest. Cook and I reworked the menus yet again for additional guests while Nan helped Aunt Charlotte and Cousin Clarissa unpack and pressed their gowns for this evening. When she helps me dress for dinner, I shall regale her with the height of Clarissa's ambition.

Poor Mr. Rockingham, repulsed without ever making an advance. Poor Clarissa, when Mr. Strickland has done with her. And, without her brother here to help her stand up to Mama, poor

Elizabeth

Wednesday, 13 October, 1813

Dearest Brother,

Are you still serving in the king's army? Do you get my letters? Since I receive no answers, sometimes I wonder if all these pages are landing on the bottom of the sea. On the slight chance that you get them, and the slighter chance that you have time to wade through them, I shall write on.

Life at Strathamsford now resembles nothing so much as a carnival. Each of us watches side shows performed by the others and at the same time performs the side shows they are watching. Tonight's whist game is only one example.

After dinner, all except Nan—who begged to be excused to finish pressing Aunt Charlotte's and Cousin Clarissa's gowns (I can't imagine why they don't travel with a maid)—gathered in the drawing room, and Mama suggested some music.

"Liza, dear," she wheedled. "You have not yet played for our guests." I looked grim, and she added encouragingly, "Perhaps a little Mozart."

Aunt Charlotte sweetly put a halt to Mama's not so subtle attempt to place me in the spotlight. "I'm sorry . . . so delicate . . . My head is just beginning . . . Clarissa might read . . ."

Uncle seemed not in the mood to be read to. "Or we might play cards," he suggested quickly.

"We had a pleasant game of whist the other night," commented Mr. Rockingham helpfully.

"Oh, do let's play whist," cried Cousin Clarissa vivaciously. "Whist is my favourite. Will you partner me, Mr. Strickland?" she cooed.

"I would not be so selfish," her choice responded. "You must play with my friend, whose recovery can only be hastened by such a lovely partner." He looked earnestly at Clarissa, trying to keep amusement out of his eyes. I thought he had gone too far, but Clarissa did not notice.

"He can play with Liza," she pouted.

"But Liza is the only one who will suffer me for a partner," Uncle fibbed.

"Wait, wait," Mr. Rockingham interrupted with a laugh. "I would welcome the chance to retire early. Please—I beg you—do not count on me to play." He held up his hand in protest as Mr. Strickland started to speak. "Another evening," he promised.

So, with the defection in our ranks, a foursome was set and Cousin Clarissa got her way after all: Mr. Strickland played her opposite. The cards fell their way, too. Had it not been for Clarissa's inept play, Uncle and I would have been soundly beaten.

In one hand, for instance, I was dealt the ace and queen of diamonds, and the card determining trumps turned up spades. Clarissa obligingly led the six of diamonds on which I played my ace to take the trick. Then I led my queen; Mr. Strickland played the king, Uncle the eight, and Clarissa the deuce of trump.

"I believe that was already our trick, Miss Whythe," Mr. Strickland said carefully.

"No, was it?" exclaimed Clarissa. "I vow I was enjoying

the company so greatly that I didn't watch the cards." She fluttered her eyelashes at her partner, who seemed unaffected by the stratagem.

"We will win only half as many tricks if we take each of them twice," he elucidated.

"You're very clever," Clarissa giggled. "I wonder why you need a man of business at all when you handle numbers so well."

Truly, Brother, if you had shared the look Uncle and I exchanged at that statement, all three of us would have disgraced ourselves by breaking into laughter.

Near the end of the evening Clarissa announced, "I'm very fond of whist. Aren't you, Mr. Strickland?"

"A well-played game is a genuine pleasure," Mr. Strickland answered, looking at neither of his opponents.

"Clarissa has enjoyed whist since . . ." commented Aunt Charlotte from the divan where she and Mama were sewing.

"Practise makes perfect," said Uncle, looking at Mr. Strickland out of the corner of his eye. Aunt Charlotte smiled happily at Clarissa, while I dropped the deck I was riffling.

"Maybe your cousin could give you instruction in the shuffle," Mr. Strickland suggested gravely. "Your brother must have neglected that part of your education." He winked perceptibly at Uncle. "Is that why you ban stakes at your card table?"

Mama sputtered at such a slur on her child. "Liza's brother taught her to riffle cards before she could read, sir," she exaggerated staunchly. "We prohibit gambling only since last winter when the vicar's son gave Liza an IOU for his next quarter's allowance."

The laughter was general. "Not Jeremy Black, your old beau?" asked Clarissa, delighted. "How could you have allowed him to lose?"

While I considered which to deny first, Jeremy's indebtedness or his status as my suitor, Uncle answered for me. "Oh, no," he said. "The unfortunate cardplayer was young William. And it may have been for the best, since Liza's brother took him in hand too, before he left for America." Uncle paused for a moment. "William is now a much improved player."

Aunt Charlotte got up from the divan with a sigh. "You make Strathamsford sound like a gaming hell rather than . . ."

"Of course," said Mr. Strickland suggestively. "One needn't play only for money."

"Why, no," agreed Clarissa, batting her eyes once again. "There are many stakes."

"Might we save the next hand for another evening?" I asked abruptly. "The hour is late, and I confess I am tired."

"I would have guessed that you enjoy risk, Miss Carlisle," Mr. Strickland tried to provoke me.

"Yes, do put the cards away," Mama said, cutting off the rejoinder of which she knew I was capable. "Will anyone join me in a tot of brandy?"

As the party broke up, Clarissa took my arm and led me toward the door. "Come, cousin," she cooed, "let us chat in my chamber before we blow out our lamps." She smiled charmingly at Mr. Strickland: "Good night, sir." She reduced her smile to polite before adding, "Good night, Aunt, Mama, Uncle."

I was barely given time to make my own farewells before I was dragged upstairs for another of Clarissa's tête-à-têtes.

"Isn't he wonderful?" she asked. I knew whom she meant. "Do you think he's smitten with me?" She didn't even pause for the answer she didn't want to hear. "Of course it's not to my credit, since there is no competition in Stratham. He *must* like me."

So there you have it, Brother. A candid appraisal of my chances on the marriage mart. No wonder I do not hang out for a husband.

I tried to ease her toward a more realistic analysis. "Do you truly wish him to court you, Clarissa?" I asked. "You scarcely know him. How can you tell if he is the sort of man who could bring you happiness?"

"A rich husband will give me happiness," Clarissa proclaimed. (Do you suppose she has been talking to Mama?)

"What of compatability of conviction and feeling?" I insisted.

"You don't think we're compatible?" she asked incredulously. "I knew at the moment I met him that we are marvelously attuned."

Lesson number two from Cousin Clarissa: marital harmony is a matter not of the emotions or the intellect but of the pocketbook. She would learn, I fear, a difficult and lengthy lesson should she manage to ensnare our razor-tongued visitor. There is a chance she does not notice the cutting edge to his conversation. Could ignorance be bliss? Certainly not for him, I believe.

Since Clarissa was not privy to my thoughts, she delivered her clincher; "Mama admires him greatly," she said.

"I'm sure she does," I replied.

"I can't decide which gown to wear tomorrow," she said dramatically. "Maybe I should consult with Mama." She stood up and shook out her skirt. "Good night, Lizzy," she trilled. I scowled. "And thank you for your help."

So now I fall into bed, exhausted. Uncle tells me he has written to you of the harvest. At any rate, most of the grain is in and the root cellar is filling up. They plan to slaughter swine for bacon and ham next week. It looks like rain.

Rascal is greatly enjoying so many people in the house. He wagged his way onto several expeditions today. And when he is ordered to stay at home, he has Mr. Rockingham for company. That is not to say he has forgotten his master. He misses you almost as much as

Your loving sister
Elizabeth

Conversation revised

Clarissa: Do let's play whist. Mr. Strickland, will you partner me?

Mr. Strickland: I would not wish to be so selfish, ma'am.

Elizabeth: Or so reckless.

Mr. S: If your cousin plays so poorly, why do you not allow gambling at your card table?

E: Out of consideration for her partner, sir.

Mr. S: But what of *your* partner? Might he not welcome easy winnings?

E: You assume too quickly, sir, that my partner is always a man. I often play with Nan Andrews.

Mr. S: What of Jeremy Black? I gather he would like to become your partner.

E: What of him, sir? I am not so single-minded as some young women.

Mr. S: There is one in particular who makes me feel like a target.

E: Ah, yes. I believe she is aiming at the jewel in your cravat.

E.

Thursday, 14 October, 1813

Dearest Brother,

Luckily the harvest was virtually complete: we are having a downpour which threatens to turn Strathamsford into a very large lake. I trust the house will remain an island.

If it does not stop soon, the rain will interfere with two new notes on our social calendar. Tomorrow night we give a dinner party and Saturday morning Mr. Strickland is to leave for business in London. By which facts you may infer that both Aunt Charlotte and Cousin Clarissa have been busy indeed.

By luncheon today the sky was grey and Mama was fretting about amusing her guests. "If it rains," she said plaintively, "we will be able to go neither to the castle this afternoon nor to market day on Saturday."

"Now, Helen," cooed Aunt Charlotte. "You plan such a gala time for your guests that royalty could not wish . . ."

Mama glowed. "It gratifies me when you enjoy your visits with us," she said.

"Really," Aunt Charlotte continued, "just a few neighbours for dinner would be more than . . ."

Mama was hooked. "Perhaps tomorrow evening," she

thought aloud. "The Blacks and Dr. and Mrs. Harrison would be seven more. We are also seven. Yes, I think we can handle fourteen."

I winced inwardly as Clarissa interrupted her musing. "Do you include Jeremy Black?" she asked. "Elizabeth's beau has been neglecting her," she announced to the company.

I could feel Mr. Strickland's gaze. "Jeremy is merely an old playmate," I said matter-of-factly. "Of course he will come to dinner. He will be glad to see you again."

"Do you think so?" asked Clarissa, thrown off the scent as I had intended. "When I saw him last, I wondered if perhaps he thought me too flirtacious."

"Surely not," said Mr. Rockingham gallantly. "Rather I would call you vivacious."

"He acted as if I had no wit," Clarissa went on, as her mother tried to signal her to leave the subject.

"Nonsense, ma'am," Mr. Strickland protested, "You have often made me laugh."

Aunt Charlotte cut off the end of his sentence with a smile that didn't reach her eyes. "If we dare not start for the castle this afternoon, what—"

"I must finish a letter to my nephew," Uncle said. "A storm will certainly put an end to any report of harvest."

"Speaking of my brother," I added, "would anyone chance a ride with me to the village?" I peered out the window at the darkening sky. "I'd like to see if there is a message from him at the post office, and I must get some paper at the stationer's." (You needn't ask, dear Brother, how I have exhausted my supply of letter paper.)

"I need you to meet with Cook to plan our dinner party, Liza," Mama said. "And the invitations must be written." She gave me a look that was almost stern.

"Please let me do the invitations for you, Aunt Helen,"

Clarissa said eagerly. "We'll go to the village another day, Liza."

"Nan mentioned lacking something at the dressmaker's," I said. "Perhaps she will go." I reached over to pat Mama's arm. "Don't worry, Mama," I soothed. "Cook and I will do your dinner proud."

"May I drive you to the village, Miss Carlisle?" Mr. Strickland asked. "Dan should have several items from the apothecary, and I also must look in at the post office." He, too, looked out the window at the sky. "If we take a carriage, we can get back more quickly and still have room for our purchases."

"My letters are ready, Giles," Mr. Rockingham said. "If you will go, please start immediately to miss the storm."

"I can swim," I said jokingly, little knowing that my Fates were paying their usual close attention.

Clarissa, who had looked crestfallen at Mr. Strickland's invitation to me, apparently decided that a hurried and probably damp excursion was not to be envied. "You are very kind to drive Liza," she said understandingly to Mr. Strickland. "May I ask you to pick up a jar of rose petal cream since you are stopping at the apothecary's?"

Mr. Strickland was about to agree when Mama answered for him. "Liza will get it for you," she said hurriedly. "It's getting darker. Do leave, if you must."

Mr. Strickland and I rose and excused ourselves from the luncheon table to fetch wraps. Clarissa was right behind me as I went to my wardrobe to get a pelisse. "Isn't he thoughtful?" she asked. I gave her no answer; she did not expect one. She prattled on while I tied my bonnet at the glass. I tried not to listen.

"Be sure to see me as soon as you return," she demanded finally. I left the chamber with only a smile in answer, and Mr. Strickland and I set off in the phaeton for the village.

"So tell me," Mr. Strickland said without preamble as we reached the lane, "about Jeremy Black."

I was caught off guard. "He is a lifelong friend, sir," I answered.

"Is he destined to become more than a friend, ma'am?" he probed.

"Not to me, sir," I said decisively.

"Does that mean you have rejected his suit?" he pried.

"A gentleman should not ask such a question," I retorted.

"Of course not," he agreed. "Have you?"

"You may ask him at dinner tomorrow evening," I said; we did not speak again until we reached the village.

The wind was rising as we accomplished our errands, conferring only about matters practical to our shopping. We hurried through the shops—I was disappointed at the post office; Mr. Strickland accepted several letters but made no sign whether or not they were welcome—and it was not until we were back in the carriage heading for home that I remembered the dressmaker's.

"I've forgotten Nan's silk," I said suddenly. "Please take me back."

"It's already starting to rain," he protested. "She'll have to get it herself." He flicked his whip at the horses. "We will be drenched if we delay now."

"Of course," I said. "What matter if Nan gets soaked." My sarcastic remark was lost, probably fortunately, in a gust of wind which made me grab for my bonnet and keep my hand firmly on top of my head. After all, he had not implied she should get it today.

"Your houseparty would make a fine melodrama," Mr. Strickland called over the storm.

"Do you think so?" I shouted in answer.

"We have all the dramatis personae," he insisted loudly.

"The injured hero," I suggested.

"His loyal friend."

"The gracious hostess."

"Her unusual daughter."

I blushed, even in the cold rain. "The treasured servants," I said, striking a blow for Nan.

"The absent brother." He ignored my thrust.

"The artistic uncle." I paused. "This cannot be called a melodrama. We have no villain."

"The interfering aunt," Mr. Strickland offered.

"Aunt Charlotte is only silly, not villainous," I protested over the wind.

"The husband-hunting cousin," he suggested.

"A villain? You are too harsh, sir." I thought for a moment. "Besides there is no dramatic action. No exits and entrances."

"I am making an exit," Mr. Strickland said. It was raining harder now and our cloaks were wetly dark.

"You are?" I asked stupidly.

"I must return to London on several business affairs," he explained. "Since Dan is unable to act for me. I should be back in under a week."

My bonnet was now limp and my hair stuck to my forehead; of course my cloak and dress were soaked through. I made no response to Mr. Strickland's announcement, and he looked over at me just as I shivered uncontrollably.

"Oh, my poor Lily," he chuckled. "You look like nothing so much as a drowned scarecrow."

My heart clenched at the intimacy of his tone as well as his words, but I kept my voice light to answer him. "Thank you, kind sir," I said. "Your words will be evergreen in my memory book." Then I shivered again.

He spoke more to himself than to me: "We should have taken shelter in the village when the rain began," he said, urging the horses to go yet faster. "But we should reach Strathamsford in another ten minutes." He opened his cloak and enfolded me under his arm. "Take my warmth until I can get you home," he ordered; he held me tightly against his chest. I confess I thought no more of cold or, if truth be told, of anything except the man embracing me. I could have wished the journey several miles longer.

And so we returned, a bedraggled pair. Mama took one look at me and hustled me off to a hot bath and bed, where I am spending a lazy evening writing to you. She did, however, permit Cook to come to my chamber after supper; and I'm glad to report that the dinner party for tomorrow night is well in hand.

Clarissa, I need not tell you, appeared in my chamber even before I got my wet clothes off. "You let him see you with your hair dripping!" she said disbelieving. "And dye from the ribbons running into your bonnet."

"It was?" I asked Nan. She nodded and motioned toward the glass. Then we both laughed. Mr. Strickland's comment made more sense when I saw the sodden creature reflected in my mirror.

Clarissa did not wait for a fuller reply. "But you don't mind, do you?" she said. "I'm so glad it was not I. Mama says that girls must look always soft and warm." She missed the look Nan and I exchanged as I went behind the screen that shielded the tub. "Did you lose your temper?" she asked hopefully.

"No," I said. She obviously had not seen me sharing Mr. Strickland's cloak.

"What did he say of me?" she called eagerly around the screen.

My mind raced in search of a truthful and not unkind answer. "He said," I paused for time, "that you are like a character in a play."

"Isn't he romantic?" asked Clarissa happily. She ran off to tell her mother.

After reflection it seems to me that I should have crushed

Clarissa's hopes of making a conquest of Mr. Strickland. You must be tired of hearing about this man. I wish I could forget the comfort of his arm around me. I do not want to like him.

Conversation revised

Mr. Strickland: Tell me about Jeremy Black.
Elizabeth: He is a childhood friend, sir.
Mr. S: Is he soon to become more than a friend?
E: We will wed at Christmas.
Mr. S: Let us turn back. The storm will begin soon, and we would be drenched.

If only you were here, Brother, we would escape to the barn loft and talk it all out. I think.

Mr. Strickland may be right: Strathamsford sounds more and more like a melodrama, doesn't it? But I think I would rather a featured role were not played by

Your loving sister,
Elizabeth

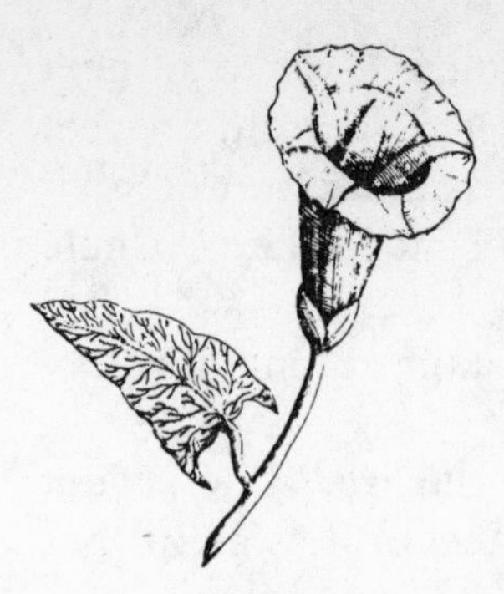

Saturday, 16 October, 1813

Dearest Brother,

He has gone. Mr. Strickland, I mean. Now perhaps life here will seem calmer. Some serenity at Strathamsford would be very welcome, especially after last night's dinner party. The dessert course was spectacular.

The occasion began auspiciously. The Harrisons arrived first, and the doctor had a private word with Mr. Rockingham, who is now managing very well with his crutches. Mrs. Harrison said as little as usual, but when the Blacks arrived, Meg moved directly to her side. (Meg will be a beautiful young woman in a year or two, Brother. Have you any thoughts in that direction?)

Mr. Strickland came in very late but seemed happy enough to chat with Clarissa in the drawing room before dinner was announced. I wondered if he knew that Clarissa had insisted on seating herself on his right hand, so he would perforce continue the conversation through the meal.

William Black, as you could guess, cornered Dr. Harrison and Mr. Rockingham for all the medical details about the latter's accident; I gather he did not quite hide his disappointment at the lack of blood. Jeremy was unable to escape Aunt Charlotte; but since I knew I was to sit next to him at dinner, thanks to Cousin Clarissa, I did not feel the least bit guilty about taking a moment with Uncle.

"Mr. Strickland goes tomorrow to London, Liza," Uncle said with concern.

"Yes, he told me," I answered, looking at him questioningly.

"He wishes to buy my painting of the fire," Uncle went on. "I've tried to persuade him to accept it as a gift, but he refuses."

"How wonderful, Uncle!" I exclaimed. "His character may leave much to be desired, but I judge his taste very good indeed."

Uncle tilted his head almost imperceptibly toward the baywindow where Clarissa trilled at her quarry. He raised one eyebrow and I laughed. "You can't blame Mr. Strickland for that tête-à-tête," I protested.

Uncle pretended I had not spoken. "What should I do about the painting, Liz?" he asked. "We're at an impasse."

"What use will he make of it?" I questioned.

"He would like it for his private collection, I gather," Uncle said. "He will deliver it to a gallery for framing while he is in London."

"Why does he not ask the gallery owner to price the picture?" I suggested. "Then you will know whether you offer a remembrance or a bounty."

"Perhaps," Uncle hesitated. "Is it permissible to look a gift horse in the mouth if one is willing to pay for it?"

I gave him a quick hug as Nan signalled to me from the hallway that dinner was served. I nodded to Mama, and our guests made their way into the dining room without overmuch prodding. As we took our places I was surprised to find myself seated between Mr. Strickland and Mr. Black, rather than between Jeremy and young William. Clarissa seemed equally startled to see her name card where I had expected mine to be. Mr. Strickland smiled serenely at Clarissa's and my confusion.

"Do you not approve the seating plan, Miss Carlisle?" he asked me quietly after Mr. Black's blessing.

"Of course, sir," I answered. "It's just that—"

"I switched the cards," he explained even more quietly. "I prefer this arrangement."

His audacity spurred my own. "Am I to take that as a compliment, sir?" I asked. "Or are you hiding behind my apron strings?" I glanced at Clarissa, who was gazing at me without charity. She turned abruptly to say something to Jeremy.

"Apron strings?" Mama repeated. She looked across Mr. Strickland to me. "You could not be wearing an apron."

"But whoever is wearing one should get accolades," said Mr. Black smoothly from my left. "The soup is superb." Mama beamed at the praise, and talk moved on to another topic.

Mr. Strickland said nothing until Mama was engaged in a conversation with Mr. Rockingham, who sat at her left hand. "You should know I needn't hide behind apron strings, Liza," he whispered.

To cover my fluster and my flushed face, I dropped my napkin to the floor. Mr. Black reached down to retrieve it for me; I thanked him; and we began to speak of Jessica. (My old friends do not hear from me so often now that my brother awaits mail call.)

Mr. Strickland joined the conversation between Mama and Mr. Rockingham, since Mrs. Harrison, who sat across from me, rarely adds comment to any discussion. The meal progressed without incident through the fish and meat courses. (Cousin Clarissa monopolised Jeremy's attention, which was not difficult since the aforementioned Mrs. Harrison sat on his other side.)

Then came the climactic dessert course. Cook and I had chosen trifle. Mama decided that each guest would add not only his own whipped cream but also his own custard. Since there was an extra bowl to pass, Nan was pressed into service to offer the whipped cream.

She was holding her bowl for Clarissa to help herself when William leaned across to peer over the rim; he was ascertaining, I'm sure, that there would be plenty left for him. All of a sudden he tapped the bowl with his elbow and—PLOP!—Clarissa acquired a lapful of whipped cream.

(I hear you laughing, Brother. But I promise it was far from funny at the time.)

"You clumsy girl!" Clarissa screeched. She pushed back her chair and stood up, which only extended the damage down the full length of her dress and onto her slippers. "Now look what you've done," she wailed.

Mama and I both rose to help, but Nan acted immediately. "I'm so very sorry," she said to Clarissa. She knelt and pushed most of the cream back into the bowl with a single downward motion of the table knife. "The stain will come out, I'm sure," she added. "I'll do it this evening."

William started to speak but his mother, who sat to his right, restrained him with her hand on his arm. "Don't worry, Miss Clarissa," she said soothingly. "Your pretty gown will be good as new."

"Are you well, Nan?" asked Dr. Harrison with concern, as Aunt Charlotte reached her daughter and put her arm around Clarissa's shoulder.

"Come, Clary," she said. "We'll just whisk you into another . . ." Clarissa's eyes began to fill with tears. "Of course in my house such a servant would be turned out with no . . ." Aunt Charlotte gave Mama a look heavy with meaning and led Clarissa from the dining room.

"Nan, please don't dwell on this," Mama reassured her. "Accidents will happen."

William shook off his mother's hand. "But it wasn't her accident, Mrs. Carlisle," he protested. "I bumped the bowl."

"Oh, William," moaned Mrs. Black.

"Oh, William," tittered Meg.

"Accidents will happen," Mama repeated. "Here's Sally with another bowl of whipped cream." She motioned Sally over to William's place. "Take extra, William."

"I couldn't eat a lick," said William miserably.

"You might bring her flowers tomorrow," Mr. Strickland suggested. "I've found flowers effective in calming angry females."

I threw him a grateful look, even as I imagined the angry females he has had occasion to calm.

"Do you think so, Liza?" William asked me.

"That's a fine idea, son," Mr. Black said, his agreement overlapping mine.

"Let me tell you, lad," said Mr. Rockingham, "about an even more embarrassing stunt I pulled when I was about your age." As he launched into an involved account of a snowball and a titled passerby, William indicated to Sally that he might consider adding whipped cream to his trifle, quite a lot of whipped cream, in fact.

Clarissa and Aunt Charlotte rejoined the party after dinner in the drawing room. Our cousin was such the center of sympathetic attention that by the time the Blacks and the Harrisons left, she was laughing off the incident.

"Goodness me," she flirted, gazing up at both Mr. Strickland and Jeremy through her eyelashes. "Where would one be without a sense of humour to maintain one's equilibrium."

(Sense of humour, indeed. She has not even apologised to Nan for her outburst. I know she hasn't because I insisted that Nan tell me.)

Dr. Harrison and Uncle exchanged glances at her statement. Mr. Strickland looked as if his trifle disagreed with him. The doctor stood and walked over to his wife, who was working her needlepoint just outside the circle of conversation. "We must be going, Mrs. Harrison," he said.

She obligingly began to gather up her wools. "Thank you for an enjoyable evening," Dr. Harrison said to Mama.

"I was glad to meet your guests," Mrs. Harrison added. "My husband had told me of them." (A two sentence farewell from Mrs. Harrison, Brother: you can assume that the occasion was a great success.)

The Blacks also made their farewells. Jeremy said he would call soon; he spoke to Mama but he looked at me. Mr. Black mentioned to Mr. Rockingham that he hoped his leg might soon permit him to come to church—our vicar was kind enough not to reveal that no one from Strathamsford has entered his sanctuary since the day of the fire.

When we were again *en famille,* so to speak, Mr. Strickland turned to Mama. "Since I leave early tomorrow, I'll take my leave of you tonight, ma'am," he said. Clarissa pretended to pout. "My gratitude for your kindness and hospitality to strangers is inexpressible," he went on.

"You know that my gratitude multiplies his," Mr. Rockingham added warmly. "Without you all," he paused to smile at Mama, "my convalescence would have been not only less rapid but also less congenial."

"You are not strangers; you have become valued friends," Mama said. "It has been our pleasure to add you to our acquaintance."

"Besides," Uncle pointed out, "were it not for our fire, Mr. Rockingham would find convalescence unnecessary. Our good turn merely attempts to equal his."

"Getting to know one another," Clarissa said significantly, "is the silver lining in the cloud of Mr. Rockingham's accident."

Mr. Strickland did not react as if meeting Clarissa was his silver lining. He gave her only a trace of a smile before asking Mama, "Is there anything I might do for you in London, ma'am?" She thought for a moment while he suggested, "A message to deliver, perhaps, or purchase of something unavailable in the country?"

"Your offer is considerate," Mama said. "But nothing comes to mind."

"I'll give you an errand for Strathamsford, if I may," Uncle said. "Could you stop by the War Office to ask for the latest news of the * * * * * * * * division?"

"Oh, yes," I said eagerly. "And take our letters to deposit there. Perhaps they will be sent on an earlier ship than if we post them here."

"Clarissa, weren't you saying . . ." prompted Aunt Charlotte.

"I have just the tiniest commission," Clarissa said obediently. "Would you bring me a pair of slippers to replace the ones which were ruined tonight?" She looked down at her feet, shod now in kidskin rather than silk. "My size is so small that I must send to London," she explained.

"Of course," agreed Mr. Strickland without enthusiasm. "You must give me the particulars." He turned to Mr. Rockingham. "You've put the packet together for me, Dan?" he asked. Mr. Rockingham nodded. "Can we go over it before you retire?"

"Certainly, Giles," Mr. Rockingham said. He reached for his crutches and asked Mama, "Will you excuse us, ma'am?" He stood and adjusted the crutches under his arms. "It has been a memorable evening."

"Unforgettable," said Uncle under his breath with a wink at me.

"Good-by and thank you again for all your kindnesses," Mr. Strickland said to Mama. "I plan to return by next week end, and will find out for you all I can about your son and his regiment."

He continued on around our circle and spoke to each of us in turn. "Thank you, too, sir," he said to Uncle. "I will try to bring you encouraging news as well."

Uncle ignored Mama's quizzical look; I gather he has

allowed Mr. Strickland to take his painting. "But I will join you for breakfast," he answered, cutting off Mama's question.

"Good-by, Mrs. Whythe," Mr. Strickland continued wryly, reaching Aunt Charlotte. "It was a happy chance that our visits coincided."

"Oh, yes," began Aunt Charlotte. "I was just telling—"

"But of course we shall see you when you return," interrupted Clarissa. "Mama says we couldn't possibly leave Strathamsford without being certain of Mr. Rockingham's recovery." She threw a dazzling smile toward the man on crutches.

"You are most compassionate," said Mr. Strickland, pro forma. "If you will give the direction of your shoemaker to the maid, I will get it at breakfast."

You see, Brother? He takes it for granted that Nan will be the last to retire and the first to rise. So I was feeling out of charity with him when at last he spoke to me.

"Good-by, Miss Carlisle," he said as the others looked on. "I shall hope to bring you good news when I return from London." He gazed at me intently. "Or at least find you in better spirits," he added.

"If you bring good news, you shall find me in better spirits, sir," I said expressionlessly. "Have a safe journey."

He questioned me with a look before he bade the company good night. Then he and Mr. Rockingham left the drawing room to review the business Mr. Strickland expected to conduct in the city.

Clarissa wished to join me in my chamber for one of her cozy chats, and Mama would have been pleased to talk over the evening; but I begged exhaustion and went straight to bed. I awoke with the dawn and about an hour later watched Mr. Strickland disappear down the lane in a drizzle. Sally had given him Clarissa's note about the slippers: I expressly forbade Nan to go downstairs this morning before nine o'clock.

As you see, I have spent much of the morning writing to you. Now I should go down myself to find Mama, so she can analyse her dinner party to a sympathetic ear. I pray that Mr. Strickland will bring recent word of you when he returns. He took with him several letters from Strathamsford which you will surely receive long before you see this long-winded account. I'd be happy with far less from you. A single line would find me giddy with excitement.

Conversation revised

Mr. Strickland: I've found flowers very effective in calming angry females.
Elizabeth: You must support a greenhouse, sir.
Mr. S: I'm glad to see that you have a sense of humour, ma'am, as your cousin recommended. But it does not seem to maintain your equilibrium.
E: Perhaps we have a family failing.
Mr. S: Shall I calm you with flowers from my greenhouse?
E: Only if it is convenient to Clarissa's shoemaker.
Mr. S: Whose direction I received from the kitchen maid. I trust Nan Andrews is well?
E: Yes, thank you. You need not bring flowers to either of us.
Mr. S: But I would hope to raise your spirits, Miss Carlisle.
E: Your departure, sir, will have that effect.

Poor Brother, to read through yet another voluminous missive and discover mere petulance. Since the source of my irritation is now removed, you can expect only rosy reports in future from

Your loving sister,
Elizabeth

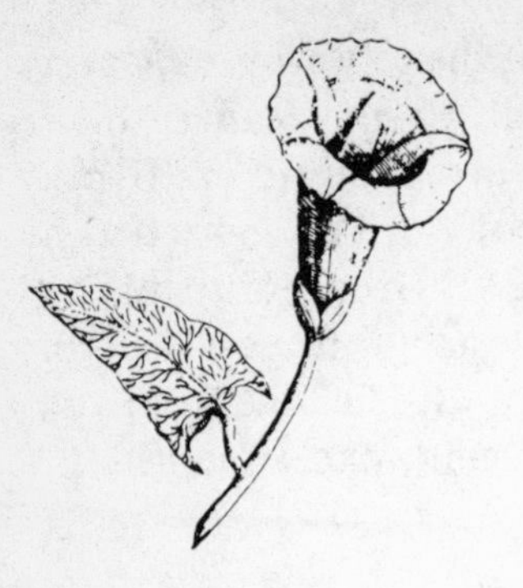

Saturday evening, 16 October, 1813

Dearest Brother,

Such an endless, dreary day. I can even find it in my heart to wish Mr. Strickland dry and warm in London. Rascal has hardly budged from the kitchen hearth; Cook quite lost her patience.

Aunt Charlotte and Cousin Clarissa did not come downstairs until luncheon, although they rang for Nan before ten o'clock, as I was drinking coffee with Mama in the breakfast room.

"Why do they need Nan?" she asked me quickly. "They are not going to rip her up about last night, are they?"

"Mama!" I exclaimed. "Such language." (I wonder, dearest Brother, where she could have heard such a vulgar expression. And why I, too, know exactly what it means.)

"Well, are they?" she asked again.

"No, Mama, I don't think so," I said. "The whipped cream fiasco gained Cousin Clarissa a good deal of attention."

"Imagine her sending Mr. Strickland to her shoemaker," Mama sputtered.

"Now, now," I soothed. "Nan is probably pressing out

others of Clarissa's gowns. All those ruffles are time-consuming,'' I added cattily.

Mama smiled. "And the ribbons,'' she said. "Just caring for her bows and sashes is a major task.'' She paused for a moment, then cried out, "Oh, Liza. She has three times as many gowns as you do. What does it matter that she's silly?''

"I'd rather have my sense than her wardrobe,'' I insisted.

"But men can't see good sense as readily as a new dress,'' Mama said firmly. "I think Nan must make up the gold silk for you right away.''

"She hasn't time,'' I protested. "Nor do I, even for fittings. We have guests in the house, you know,'' I added pettishly.

"Nonsense,'' said Mama. "Your needs come first. Where are the style books?''

"Mama,'' I said. "A gold silk gown will not get me a husband.'' Mama frowned. "Nor would I want one whose main gift was an eye for colour,'' I added.

"The important goal is marrying a good man,'' Mama said. "You can learn to love him later.''

"Just because it came out well for you does not mean it will come out well for me,'' I pleaded.

"Nonsense,'' Mama repeated. "Mutual attraction is a poor basis for a happy marriage.''

"Are we discussing Jeremy Black yet again?'' I asked suspiciously.

"He is a good man,'' Mama hedged.

"Yes, he is that,'' I agreed. "Might we be discussing our guests as well?''

"You must admit they are personable,'' Mama said. "Mr. Strickland is a bit stiff, it's true; but Mr. Rockingham could not be more pleasant.''

"Ah, but are they good men?'' I asked. "They could be footpads for all we know.''

"Not footpads,'' Mama protested. "They have horses.''

"You know what I mean." I laughed. "We have only their word for who and what they are."

"When you're my age, dear," Mama said, "you'll know how to judge character." She looked at me to see if I would answer her in your decrepit "when you're my age" voice, but I disappointed her.

"That will be helpful, Mama," I said obediently.

"Besides," she went on, "you must have had several talks with Mr. Strickland." She thought for a moment. "You and he seem to share secret jokes." Her tone turned disapproving. "I think more reserve is becoming to a young woman."

"But I have no thought of fixing his regard," I said at once. "Truly, we disagree more often than not."

"Surely you do not argue with him!" Mama wailed. "Clarissa would never do that."

"No," I agreed. "She never would."

"Clarissa arranged last night's seating," Mama commented, her attention deflected. "I confess I was surprised to see that she seated Mr. Strickland at your left rather than hers."

"Clarissa was surprised too," I couldn't resist saying. Just then Nan came in and rescued me from the necessity of an explanation. "It was the ruffles, wasn't it?" I asked her. "You've pressed a mile and a half of ruffles."

"Good morning, Mrs. Carlisle," Nan answered. "No, I'm certain it was over two miles."

"What will she wear this evening?" Mama questioned. She continued without waiting for Nan's answer. "I think Liza must have a gown from the gold silk as soon as possible. Surely that presents no difficulty?" She smiled enchantingly at Nan, who can resist her as little as you and I can.

"Of course not," Nan replied, careful not to look in my direction. "Let me bring you the style books after luncheon."

"We might turn through them right now," Mama suggested; and Nan went to fetch them. So I am to have a new gown. I chose as simple a design as Mama would approve, but of course such a momentous decision took the rest of the morning.

Mama is writing to you, too, so I have been permitted to spend the evening with a writing board on my lap. Mr. Rockingham would be reading except that Clarissa is chattering at him. Uncle is sketching the domestic scene, which includes a dog who moved to the drawing room hearth when the kitchen fire was banked for the night.

Only one figure is missing. Well, perhaps two are lacking. One thing is sure: the days were far from tedious when either of the two gentlemen I have in mind stayed at Strathamsford.

Your sister loves you.
Elizabeth

Conversation revised

Mama: They are not going to rip her up about last night, are they?

Elizabeth: I don't think so. Remember the ruffles.

Mama: Yes, I've decided Nan must make up the gold silk for you.

E: She has not the time to sew even one ruffle, let alone an entire gown.

Mama: Nonsense. A simple gown will be adequate.

E: To catch a simple husband, Mama?

Mama: Why is it that you cannot like Jeremy Black? He is a good man.

E: Good and simple, I vow.

Mama: Mr. Strickland is not simple.

E: No, I confess I find him quite complex. But a good man?

Mama: When you're my age, dear, you'll be older.
E: Yes, Mama . . . and better able to judge character.
Mama: Does he not whisper to you when you are in company?
E: Only to vex me.
Mama: Surely you have not revealed your temper to him!
E: A daughter of yours would not dare to.
Mama: Certainly a niece of mine would not.
E: Not unless someone spilled whipped cream on her ruffles.

And, Brother, I fear I must yet answer charges about the place cards. Such injured innocence is your

E.

Sunday evening, 17 October, 1813

Dearest Brother,

This morning was radiant, the first sunshine since before Thursday's storm. We were all in high spirits; at breakfast Mr. Rockingham said that if it was not too troublesome, he would like very much to hear Mr. Black's sermon. (The poor man has not been beyond the terrace since he arrived: he must absolutely crave new vistas.) So we went to church.

It was, of course, a complex undertaking. Uncle believes that our old landau has the most gentle ride, so Sally was sent to tell Jem to give the carriage a quick dusting. Has the landau been out at all since Papa died? The leather hoods, I was dismayed to see, are cracked and brittle; we must send the carriage to the coachmaker before we use it on a cloudy day.

Nan brought bolsters from the box room to support Mr. Rockingham's injured leg. When Uncle and I saw how the cushions filled the inside of the carriage, we decided to ride alongside rather than crowd the passengers.

While Mama and Aunt Charlotte adjusted their bonnets at the looking glass, Clarissa took the pillows with only a nod to Nan—she still has mentioned neither her outburst on Friday evening nor the change of place cards. She adjusted and readjusted the padding as Mr. Rockingham came slowly down the front steps with Uncle on one side and me on the other in case he lost his balance. Then, as he negotiated the step into the landau, she proprietarily offered her arm.

Cousin Clarissa has apparently, in the absence of the former object of her attention, appointed herself custodian of Mr. Rockingham's comfort. "Are you quite at ease, Mr. Rockingham? Would you like another cushion? Let me take your crutches for you." And I was able to overhear only her comments before the carriage set off for church. I confess I did not regret I had determined to ride.

Clarissa even looked pleased that because of the space taken up by the bolsters she was wedged against Mr. Rockingham on the seat. Gracious, Brother, he is old enough to be her father. Surely she does not hope to attach him?

She was still all solicitude when the four debarked from the carriage at Christ Church. I gather from Aunt Charlotte's complaisance and Mama's annoyance that Clarissa's concern had continued at full tilt. Mr. Rockingham was courteous to her, but he seemed to me to be eager to manage on his own.

Our party caused quite a stir, I needn't tell you, as we entered the churchyard. Mrs. Black bustled over from the group of friends she was no doubt entertaining with a report of our recent dinner party. She clucked over Mr. Rockingham and cooed toward Clarissa and chattered at Mama and Aunt Charlotte: you'd have thought she made up the congregation all by herself. I'm afraid I heard an invitation to dinner amongst the nonsense. Jeremy, of course, was not far behind his mother; he hovered over me until he handed me into our pew.

Dr. Harrison left his own pew as we entered the church and came over to greet Mr. Rockingham; Mrs. Harrison stayed, you can guess, in her seat, but she smiled shyly at our party.

Mr. Black's sermon for the twenty-fourth Sunday after Trinity was both long and complex; you would have been edified, I am sure. I am not so certain that Mr. Rockingham found it as pleasing in actuality as in anticipation. But perhaps he only seemed to doze off. He complimented Mr. Black with apparent sincerity at the door after the service.

Many of the congregation remembered Aunt Charlotte and Cousin Clarissa from earlier visits to Strathamsford, and everyone was curious to meet the stranger injured during the fire. So we spoke to all in the churchyard. The Ludlows were particularly eager to speak with Mr. Rockingham and to see for themselves that he is mending rapidly. Clarissa and her mother were reserved in their company, but the rest of us were obviously pleased to show off his progress.

Mr. Strickland, no doubt, would have forgotten who they are. Funny, not one person asked after him. Perhaps Mrs. Black had already spread the news of his departure.

Our trip home reversed the journey to church, with Clarissa solicitous and Mr. Rockingham independent. When we arrived back at Strathamsford, Mr. Rockingham appeared relieved; and he asked to rest before dinner. The rest of us endured Clarissa's effusions on our reception in the village and about Mr. Rockingham's fortitude in attending the service.

I'm sorry to report that Mama's wineglass was full throughout dinner, but afterwards she took a nap while Nan and I escaped to walk with Rascal through the beech grove. The leaves' brilliance is reaching its height and the recent rains have only intensified the effect. Nan and I giggled like old times and Rascal romped like a puppy—a very large puppy.

There was no escape, however, after supper. All but Nan gathered for coffee in the drawing room.

"You're sure the day has not overtaxed your strength, Mr. Rockingham?" fretted Clarissa, bending over his chair.

"She is always thinking of other . . ." said Aunt Charlotte dotingly to no one in particular.

"Truly I wish to forget my affliction," declared Mr. Rockingham. "You all must be as wearied of it as I."

"You never mention it, sir," said Mama, with only the slightest emphasis on the first word. Uncle and I exchanged glances but restrained our smiles; Mama was obviously herself once more. "How shall we fill the evening?" Mama continued. "Some music? Elizabeth, will you play?"

"If you wish it, Mama," I said, resigned. You know Mama, Brother. She has always considered my talent worthy of the concert stage even though it is hardly sufficient for the nursery.

"Music would be delightful," said Mr. Rockingham, who seemed happy to have the subject changed.

"Indeed," said Uncle, my other nondiscerning admirer.

"While you play, Lizzy," Aunt Charlotte began, "Clarissa can leaf through your music to find the more difficult . . ."

Mama and Uncle both turned to glare at Aunt Charlotte, but I was glad to show Clarissa to the music shelf. And truly, Brother, you would have been vastly amused. Aunt Charlotte could not wait for Clarissa to display her musical gift, and interrupted me halfway through my unpretentious repertoire. Yet when Clarissa was finally seated at the spinet, our aunt realised that Mr. Rockingham was free to converse with Mama or me. As a result she was far more irked than when I was the center of attention. She soon commandeered the chair next to Mr. Rockingham and spent the rest of the evening remarking to him on the nuances of excellence in Clarissa's performance.

I felt quite sorry for him.

But I did not come to his aid; instead I began this letter to you, which I am finishing in my bedchamber.

Conversation revised

Clarissa: You are sure the day has not overtaxed you, Mr. Rockingham?

Mr. Rockingham: Actually, I am exhausted.

Aunt Charlotte: But if you retire, you will not be able to hear Clarissa—

Mr. Strickland: Exactly.

Mr. R: I'm sure she is very accomplished.

Elizabeth: Yes, she accomplishes what she will, and plays the spinet very prettily too.

You see, Brother? I must stop revising conversations. Not only am I stooping to easy insult but I am also including absent persons. Why did Mr. Strickland jump into my revision? He has not been in the thoughts of

Your loving sister,
Elizabeth

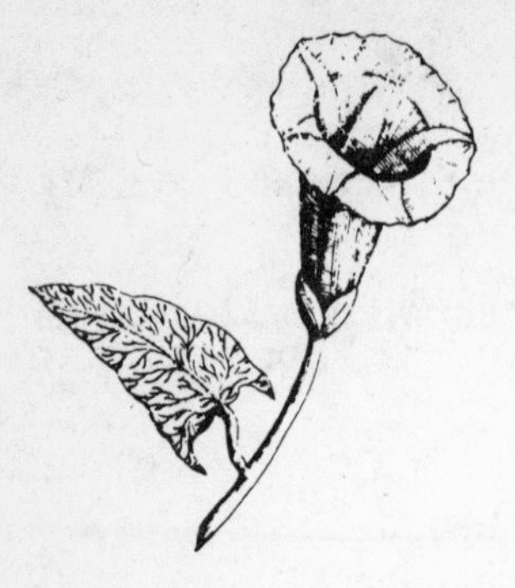

Monday afternoon, 18 October, 1813

Dearest Brother,

How is everything with you? It is nonsensical, I suppose, to ask a soldier if he has congenial companions. But we would certainly welcome your company here, not that we are bored.

Last night after our musical evening, Clarissa had her cozy chat not with me but with her mother. This morning our cousin set forward ambitious proposals for the day's entertainment.

"Since the coach is ready, why don't we take a picnic to the cathedral?" she said vivaciously. "The brasses there are lovely and the weather could not be more perfect."

"What a wonderful . . ." said Aunt Charlotte, sounding almost but not quite spontaneous.

"Do you think it wise for Mr. Rockingham to attempt such a long ride so soon after his first outing?" Mama asked. "And Cook can be difficult when we give her short notice."

"Our picnic at the Rose and Crown was the highlight of my stay there," said Mr. Rockingham obligingly.

"Oh, you've already had a picnic," pouted Clarissa.

"Elizabeth has promised to pose for me this morning,"

Uncle fibbed convincingly. "I am eager to paint her russet riding habit against the foliage in the woodlot." He gave me an encouraging nod. "So she could not join an expedition to the cathedral in any case."

"But I thought we had agreed," I replied with as much truth as Uncle, "to wait until I had untangled the September ledgers. Harvest season is confusing enough when the accounts are current." I grimaced.

"Perhaps I could take a look?" offered Mr. Rockingham hopefully. "My mind feels as out of shape as my leg, and with Giles acting as his own man of business, I have little cause to exercise it."

"Oh, could you?" I exclaimed. "My knowledge is meagre—"

"Must we postpone our sitting to review the bookkeeping system?" asked Uncle glumly.

"No, no," said Mr. Rockingham. "Why not let me look over the books, and tomorrow you can answer my questions." His happiness at the prospect of useful employment appeared to be balanced by the dismay of Cousin Clarissa and Aunt Charlotte at having him solitarily occupied.

"We would greatly appreciate your advice," Mama said. "My son's regiment was called up so abruptly that he had time to give no more than scant instruction to his sister."

"If I could teach her all I know," said Mr. Rockingham quietly to Mama, "it would not begin to repay your hospitality to a stranger."

Mama smiled warmly at him. "I protest, sir," she said. "Call it instead help for a friend."

"I think numbers are tedious," Clarissa interrupted petulantly.

"Your talents are more feminine than . . ." said Aunt Charlotte smugly.

"I am entirely hopeless with numbers myself," said

Mama, trying to make peace. "But Elizabeth seems quite to enjoy them."

"I might if I knew what I was about," I agreed. "Let me fetch the account books."

"Would you like to shop in the village this afternoon?" Mama asked Aunt Charlotte and Cousin Clarissa. "Mrs. Black told me yesterday that the dressmaker has received a new shipment of French silks." The two were allowing themselves to be cajoled into an expedition when I left to get the ledgers and to change into my russet riding habit.

Uncle and I spent a delightful Clarissa-less morning. Rascal, of course, came with us and enjoyed it almost as much as we did. (He shared lunch.) I posed in front of the tall oak by the south meadow; our uncle makes good on his threats.

When I had been standing in the same position for what felt like weeks, I said to Uncle, "Perhaps you should restrict your artistic efforts to still lifes."

Uncle stood back to study the drawing pad on his easel. "People are much more interesting, don't you think?" he asked.

"Some I find quite dull," I said, breaking my pose to take a step and stretch out my arms. Rascal, who decided that I was ready for a romp, dashed across the meadow and jumped on me to show that he, too, was ready to play. I now have muddy paw prints decorating my new riding habit; you would no doubt find it most becoming.

Uncle ignored your dog and agreed with my statement. "Tedious, you might call some," he said.

"You couldn't possibly refer to my cousin, Uncle dear?" I said. "Or her mother?" I sat on the old stone wall.

Uncle spoke to the sketch on his easel. "The young lady surely does not consider our masculine visitors wearisome."

"You can't talk to your drawing," I said indignantly. "It's a drawing of me."

"I was talking to Rascal," Uncle said self-righteously.

"Wasn't I, boy?" Your beloved dog rushed over to Uncle, whose jacket soon matched my habit in decoration. "Down, dog!" Uncle said sternly, but Rascal paid no attention. (Need I tell you that?)

"She didn't answer, dog," Uncle continued, brushing at the mud with one hand and holding Rascal down with the other. "I wouldn't call them wearisome, anyway." He thought for a moment. "Mr. Rockingham perhaps lacks a cutting edge, but I find Mr. Strickland a diverting man."

"Clarissa does not find Mr. Rockingham dull," I said.

"And Elizabeth apparently does not find Mr. Strickland diverting," said Uncle.

"You are obviously intrigued by him," I retorted. "Why do we not speak, for instance, of Aunt Charlotte?"

"Because she is tedious," said Uncle. "Will you resume your pose?"

"You're really going to paint me?" I asked.

"You'll be famous," he answered.

"Portrait of a woman with mud on her gown," I said. I stood again by the oak as Uncle had requested. "Do you think they'll hang me in the National Gallery?"

Uncle concentrated on his work. "Or in the stables," he said.

"Rascal," I said, "your pawprints are funnier than some people's witticisms."

"Probably she means the tiresome Clarissa," Uncle remarked to his sketch.

"Of course," I said.

We returned to Strathamsford early in the afternoon. Since Mr. Rockingham is again closeted with the ledgers and Mama and the Whythes have not yet returned from the village, I have seen no one but Nan. Wait—I hear the carriage.

Mama reports that the shopping excursion was a success: Aunt Charlotte found the wools she wished for her embroidery and Clarissa brought herb teas for Mr. Rockingham. Poor man: he will not be allowed to drink simple Earl Grey so long as she is here to decide what he should like.

Nan pretends she is not speaking to Rascal, since she's the one who must spend the afternoon cleaning both my riding habit and Uncle's jacket. When she remembers where she put the velvet-brusher. She sends regards. I told her she should write to you herself and she blushed. You'd think I had suggested she correspond with Mr. Strickland.

Now I'm off to interrupt Mr. Rockingham at his labours. I probably should have written this letter in the library, so that he could have asked me questions as he found items which require explanation. I warrant there are far more entries to puzzle him than when you managed the accounts. Couldn't you tell General Ross that you are needed at home?

I retract that last statement. Of course all members of the king's army are needed at home.

But I'm no longer revising conversations. Did you notice?

Love from
Elizabeth

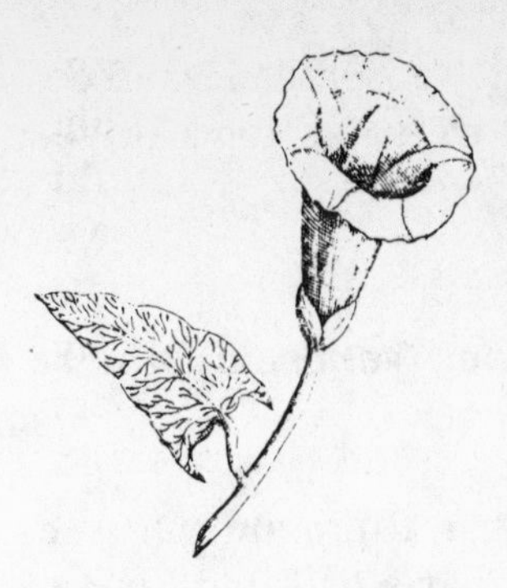

Late Monday evening, 18 October, 1813

Dearest Brother,

I believe I mentioned in this afternoon's report that I expected to join Mr. Rockingham in the library? As I was putting your letter with the other mail for the village on the hallway table, I heard a carriage drive up to the front door. Of course I ducked into the drawing room to peek out the window: it was Jeremy, wearing a new cape and looking fit to adorn a five pound note.

I swear, Brother, if I were as good-looking as Jeremy my letter paper would bear a crest. On the other hand, if I were as self-involved as Jeremy, I couldn't write a letter that anyone would wish to read. So you must be satisfied with plain stock.

Perhaps you can tell that I am not eager to continue with my story. But I shall plunge onward.

Conversation unrevised

Jeremy: Would you care (sniff sniff) to go for a drive, Elizabeth?

Elizabeth: Another time, perhaps. I was just about—

Mama (joining us in the hallway): Nonsense, Liza. You have nothing pressing. She'd love to go for a drive, Jeremy.

E: I'll get my pelisse, Mama.

(Later)

J: Have you recovered fully from your (sniff sniff) illness of last week, Elizabeth?

E: Yes, thank you. I am quite well.

J: I knew you were not yourself that afternoon. Or our (sniff sniff) little talk would have had a different conclusion.

E: Please, Jeremy. I hope to keep you as my friend. I do not wish for a closer tie.

J: You have not yet sampled a closer tie. (Grabs E; kisses her.)

E: (Pushes him away; slaps him so loudly that the horses are startled.) Do Not Do That Again.

J: (Rubs red handprint on cheek after team is calm.) Is this how you mean to treat your betrothed?

E: Jeremy, you will never know how I treat my betrothed. Take me home.

It was awful—the kiss, I mean. It reminded me of nothing so much as pressing my lips to a fish: wet, flaccid, and replusive. If that's kissing, I'm glad to be on the shelf.

Then, to prolong my discomfort, Mama insisted he stay to dinner. You will be relieved to know that I have successfully expunged this evening from my memory.

It is just now—endlessly—over.

Good night from
your weary
Elizabeth

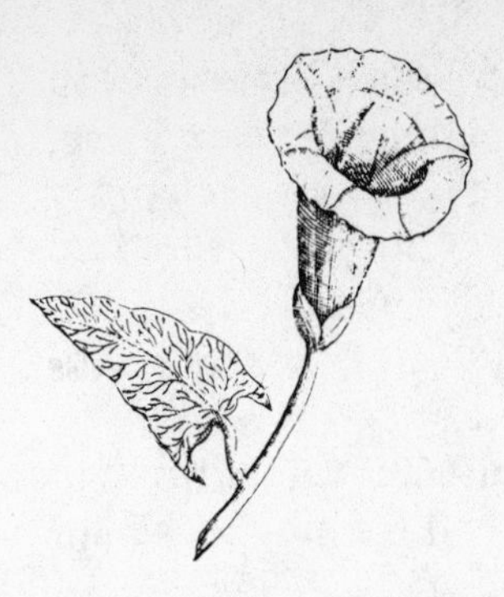

Early Wednesday morning, 20 October, 1813

Dearest Brother,

However are you spending your evenings in the New World? Not writing letters to the Old World, I'll be bound. Of course you have other obligations, but never forget that your most solemn duty is to come safely home. Then, if you can find a moment, write to those from Strathamsford who haunt the post office.

It is dawn, a grey dawn. But I could sleep no longer: I retired very early last evening. Why, you ask, did I retire so early? I retired early because I was falling asleep over Clarissa's reading aloud. Truly, never before have I found Shakespeare numbing. You can guess who suggested that Clarissa entertain the company. (You can also guess that a week with our relatives has robbed me of what little charity I possessed heretofore.)

It is my opinion that Aunt Charlotte proposed Clarissa's reading to head off another game of whist, which she had suggested the night before. You no doubt remember, as she obviously did not, that our Clarissa does not show to best advantage at the card table.

"You might play . . ." she said Monday evening after dinner.

"Oh, do let's have a game of whist," said Clarissa excitedly. "We haven't played but once since I came." She glanced around at the rest of us, but no one else mirrored her enthusiasm. "Although I suppose," she pouted, "there will be no stakes."

"Only her credit as a whist player," Uncle whispered to me.

Mr. Rockingham and I spoke simultaneously, although only one of us was glaring at Uncle. "I'd enjoy a game," said Mr. Rockingham politely.

"A pleasant evening is stakes enough," I said.

"One we must be prepared to lose," said Uncle in the lull as both Mr. Rockingham and I waited for others to repeat his comment.

"Yes, prepare to lose," Clarissa said gaily. "Mr. Rockingham and I will triumph over all challengers."

Uncle winked at me as Mama made a rare recommendation. "Perhaps you should cut the deck for partners," she said.

"Oh, Clarissa and Mr. Rockingham make such a nice . . ." said Aunt Charlotte. I nearly choked. Even Mama coughed once.

"Uncle always plays with Liza anyway; he said so." Clarissa overruled any adjustment to her plans. "Nan isn't here to get the table?"

Mama, Uncle, and I jumped to our feet as one; and with far too many cooks for such a simple broth, the table was set up and the game begun. Mama, since she was on her feet, poured herself a glass of ratafia.

I will spare you, dear Brother, a full-scale narrative of Clarissa's play at whist. Suffice it to say that she giggled about not counting trumps, shrugged helplessly at her partner after playing the wrong suit, and once even forgot which suit was trumps. (Our cousin thinks it unladylike to know one number from another but not, apparently, to lose her partner's money: if only we had been playing for real money, I could be ordering a fur-lined pelisse from London instead of writing another dreary letter to you.)

Still and all, the game proceeded smoothly until Clarissa wondered aloud whether to play her king or her knave of trump, and even the sweet-tempered Mr. Rockingham became exasperated.

"If you announce your hand, Miss Whythe," he said with the merest trace of acrimony, "our opponents will find it even less difficult to empty our purses." Clarissa's mouth dropped open at the shock of a reprimand. "Are you quite well?" he continued, when her stunned expression did not alter.

"Why, yes, I feel fine, sir," Clarissa managed to say. "And you?"

"You're more tired than . . ." said Aunt Charlotte to her daughter. She looked to the rest of us for confirmation. "Clarissa gets these headaches and . . ." she went on, giving her daughter a glance heavy with meaning.

"Am I playing foolishly?" Clarissa asked Mr. Rockingham with a disbelieving smile. "It must be my head. Do you think it best that I retire, Mama?"

"You must take care not to overtax . . ." said Aunt Charlotte sympathetically.

"Would you be gracious enough to excuse me?" Clarissa spoke to Mr. Rockingham. "I'm sorry to break up the game," she simpered as she stood up. "You won't be able to play without me."

"We'll send for Nan to take your hand," said Uncle decisively. "Please do not feel you have spoiled our evening."

"I'll walk upstairs with you," I said, "and see if Nan is willing to play." The others bid Clarissa good night.

"She'll play if you tell her to," said Clarissa sullenly as we left the room.

"Of course she would," I agreed. "I only hope she will play if I ask her to."

"I vow I do not understand why you treat your servants with so much regard," Clarissa protested. "Mama says it only makes them hard to handle."

"I hope you are rested in the morning," I said as we reached the door to her bedchamber. I felt as weary as she claimed to be.

We exchanged good nights, and I went on to climb to Nan's room on the third floor.

"Come in," she called to my knock at her door.

"Clarissa pleaded the headache after she finally goaded Mr. Rockingham into criticising her play at whist," I explained. "We all hope you will consent to take her cards."

Nan was writing at her desk. "I don't believe it," she said, looking up. "Mr. Rockingham?"

"The poor man was tried beyond endurance," I said. "Tonight she announced her honours in trumps. Won't you come down?"

"You really think I should?" Nan asked.

"Certainly I do," I replied, and handed her a hairbrush. "Run this through your hair and come with me."

Nan allowed herself to be coaxed to the drawing room, and when we entered, Mr. Rockingham said to her, "I'm glad you have agreed to be my partner, Nan." He smiled warmly. "We weren't ready to put away the table."

Nan looked startled and turned to me. "I'm not to be your partner, Liza?" she asked.

"Don't worry, my dear," Uncle reassured her. "My nephew taught you to play cards as well as his sister does." He picked up the deck of cards in the middle of the table. "I think it's my riffle and my partner's deal."

Thus our game was hardly interrupted by the change in players, except that no one spoke except between hands for upwards of an hour. Bored by the lack of chatter, Aunt Charlotte declared that she too would retire. "Perhaps I'll go . . ." she said as she gathered up her needlepoint and replaced it in her sewing bag. "Clarissa gets her constitution from . . ."

"Would you like me to ask Cook for some warm milk?" Mama asked. "Or a tisane for your headache?"

"Thank you, no," Aunt Charlotte said. "Rest is the best . . ."

Those of us at the card table simply smiled our good nights. After Aunt Charlotte left, even Mama became involved in the card playing: she watched Mr. Rockingham's hand and studied his moves. She seemed to lose her thirst after the Whythes left the party.

When we finally quit the table it was past midnight. Uncle and Mr. Rockingham stayed on to sip a brandy, but Mama, Nan, and I went directly upstairs to bed. Nan came into my chamber, of course, to help me out of my gown and to braid my hair. I was tying my winter robe tightly—the nights are colder now—when she said, "Mr. Rockingham seems a gentleman."

"Yes," I said. "I like him very much."

"As does Clarissa," Nan continued.

"Alas, yes," I agreed. "If only she were less transparent."

"He handles her graciously," Nan commented. "But it is your mother whose company he welcomes."

"Truly I had not seen him out of patience with Clarissa until tonight," I went on. Then what she had said about Mama registered in my mind. "Do you think so, Nan? About Mama?" I asked. Nan smiled. "I hadn't noticed," I admitted. "But I'll be more observant from now on."

My observations, however, will have to wait. This ends abruptly because Nan is on her way to the village and tells me that she must stop at the post office anyway. Uncle and I are promised to spend the morning with Mr. Rockingham and the ledgers. So, dear Brother, be prepared at your return for a mathematically accomplished

Elizabeth

Thursday afternoon, 21 October, 1813

Dearest Brother,

At long last I have deduced why we receive no letters from America: you are favouring someone else with your correspondence. I've guessed, haven't I? I wonder who she is. She's keeping very quiet about her mail. Seriously, Brother, I insist that you write me a letter. If I receive nothing from you in the next week, I shall send nothing the week after that. (Now if only you will believe that I have turned hard-hearted in your absence . . . .)

Did I tell you that Uncle and I were to work yesterday morning on the books with Mr. Rockingham? The session had been postponed from earlier in the week for reasons only slightly more tedious than the news you are accustomed to reading in my handwriting.

I entered the breakfast room earlier than usual to find Mama and Mr. Rockingham chatting companionably over coffee. (Perhaps Nan is right?)

"Good morning, Liza," Mama said as I went to her chair to kiss her cheek. "You're up with the birds today."

"Good morning, Mama, Mr. Rockingham," I replied. "Then I gather that you woke the birds?"

"Good morning, Miss Carlisle," said Mr. Rockingham.

"Surely you do not expect to find the early bird's worm in the accounts." (Have you noticed, Brother, how breakfast wit often seems forced?) He turned to Mama. "We're beginning revision of the ledgers today," he said, "your brother and your daughter with me."

"You are wise, sir, to exclude your hostess," Mama said with a smile. "Numbers have always rattled around in my head."

"Now, Mama," I protested. "You can figure the yards of silk for a gown faster than the dressmaker."

"That's not mathematics," Mama insisted. "That's needlework."

Mr. Rockingham and I burst out laughing. "We would be pleased to have you join us, ma'am," Mr. Rockingham said. "They also serve who only stand and—uh—watch."

"Watch? Watch what?" asked Uncle as he came into the breakfast room. "Good morning, all. May I watch too?"

"No, you can't," I said. "We're discussing our session with the ledgers, and you must be a participant, not a spectator." I paused to take a breath and added, "Good morning."

Mama and Mr. Rockingham nodded in greeting. "Was this the day we were to work on the accounts?" Uncle asked, his tone plaintive.

"You know it is, Uncle," I said energetically. "So as soon as you've eaten, we can get started."

"Oh," Uncle said. He helped himself to a very large breakfast from the sideboard. "I'll rush to join you," he drawled, dishing up his eggs very deliberately.

"Come now, sir," Mr. Rockingham said. "You must view the ledgers with your artistic eye. Orderly accounts have a symmetry, truly they do." Uncle looked dubious. "Perhaps no one has shown it to you before," he went on.

"No," Uncle answered between unhurried bites of a biscuit dripping with honey. "No one has."

"Symmetry?" Mama asked. "I believe I should like to

see that." Mr. Rockingham smiled. "Can you explain it before the Whythes are ready to visit the lending library?"

Uncle and I looked at each other. "Yes!" we said in unison.

Mr. Rockingham reached for his crutches. "Shall we adjourn to the library?" he said to Mama.

Uncle's plate was still heaped with bacon and crumb cake. "You may start without me," he said regretfully. "I'll come as quickly as I am able." He poured himself another cup of coffee and carefully added sugar and cream.

Mama held the door as Mr. Rockingham awkwardly got to his feet. "Don't be long, Brother," she said to Uncle. "We must not abuse our guest's generous offer." The two of them left the breakfast room and I pushed their chairs under the table, disturbing the dog who was hiding there. Then I, too, went to the door as Uncle spoke to Rascal, who emerged hoping to share Uncle's feast.

"That man is going to demonstrate the artistry of bookkeeping," he explained to the animal. "Then you can teach me to bark at the moon."

I scowled over my shoulder and let the door close behind me with what you would have to call a slam.

Our morning, however, was truly enthralling. I had thought that Mr. Rockingham would merely go over columns upon columns of figures, but we hardly discussed figures at all. He recommends that we revise completely the manner in which we estimate yield and profitability. He has offered to help set up the records and will write everything down for you. I know you will be as fascinated as I: symmetry, that's what it is.

Uncle arrived in the library well into Mr. Rockingham's explanations, as our guest was showing Mama and me how he had used the old map of the area to estimate approximate acreage of our various parcels.

"Is this the best map we have?" Uncle asked disbelieving. "I thought the village was surveyed several years ago when Dr. Harrison deeded a farm to his son."

"Yes, it was surveyed, Uncle," I agreed. "The records are in the large locked drawer of the desk." I thought for a moment. "But Papa was sick then. I don't think a new map was ever made."

Uncle was already unlocking the drawer. "No new map?" he asked as he searched through the papers. "I'll get started right away." He found the sheets he was looking for and left the room at once. And that, dear Brother, is the last we shall see of our Uncle in the library until his new map of Strathamsford has been completed. Do you not concur?

Mama and I remained until time for luncheon; we arranged with Mr. Rockingham to continue our planning soon. I have made a list of questions for Peter Smith about the farms, but both Mama and I acted the gracious hostesses all the afternoon to Aunt Charlotte and Cousin Clarissa to make up for ignoring them all the morning.

We are promised to the Blacks for dinner. Clarissa plans to astound the company with yet another of her pale ruffled confections; you can guess how Nan spent the afternoon. Mama is insistent that I wear my new gold silk, although the gown is only basted together. Nan had hoped to work on it after luncheon. Perhaps Mama will agree to my blue crepe. (I shall remind her that Jeremy admired it when I wore it last.)

A snippet of gold silk is enclosed with

love from
Elizabeth

Late evening, Thursday, 21 October, 1813

Dearest Brother,

Unless you were in the midst of full-scale battle, you had a calmer evening tonight than I. (I truly think a skirmish with the Americans would not begin to measure up.) My new gown was a disaster, Clarissa misjudged her chances with Mr. Rockingham, he lost his temper after Mama took too much wine, and Jeremy was insufferable. To top it off, Mr. Strickland has returned and I am furious with him.

But I'll muddle it hopelessly if I don't start at the beginning.

You have inferred that Mama remained adamant about the gold silk gown. "I refuse to let you be overshadowed by your cousin," she declared. "She will hover over one and flirt with the other, and no one will notice you at all unless you wear something new."

"They'll notice me if my dress falls off," I said.

"That's nonsense," Mama insisted. "Just be careful to move gently. All you need do is remember you're a lady, and there could be no trouble." (Mark her words, dear Brother. The Fates certainly did.)

She was also wrong about Clarissa flirting with Jeremy—our cousin barely bade him good evening—but all too right about her hovering over Mr. Rockingham. I was disgusted. Dinner conversation consisted mainly of Clarissa asking, "Wouldn't you like a little more potato, Mr. Rockingham?" and Mr. Rockingham answering, "I'd rather you didn't bother yourself," and Mama saying, "I believe I'll take another glass of wine."

Mrs. Black did not quite conceal her fascination. I hope something exciting happens elsewhere in Strathamshire soon, or her account of this dinner will be all over the county by the end of next week.

In the interests of accurate reporting I must admit that Mama was wobbling a little as we removed from the dining room. Uncle took her elbow when she stumbled over the doorsill to the drawing room.

"Why don't you sit over here, Helen," he suggested, guiding Mama toward a settee. "I'll get you some coffee."

"Meg, dear," Mrs. Black asked her daughter, "get the tray so I can pour for Mrs. Carlisle."

"May I get a cup for you, Mr. Rockingham?" Clarissa simpered.

Mama sank into the couch and glared weakly at Clarissa. "I think I'd prefer a snifter of brandy," she said a trifle thickly.

"Are you sure you're . . . ?" asked Aunt Charlotte.

You would have thought from Clarissa's behaviour that Mr. Rockingham had gratefully accepted her offer. She bustled over to the settee and handed him a cup and saucer; then she held out a plate of minted candies. "A sweet, sir?" she cooed.

Mr. Rockingham turned his back on Clarissa as if she had not spoken to him and made his way to Mama's side. "I'm having coffee," he said. "Won't you join me?"

Without even looking at Clarissa, Mama reached out to push the plate away, and candies scattered all over the Turkey carpet. I dropped to my knees to pick them up as Mama apologised to Mrs. Black for her clumsiness. Meg crawled under the spinet to reach a candy that had skidded across the bare floor, and Jeremy decided that the Carlisles needed his rescue.

"Liza told me earlier that her mother has not been well," he explained pompously and untruthfully.

"I do hope it is nothing serious," intoned Mr. Black, projecting as if to the back of the church.

That's when young William came over to the settee to peer closely at Mama. "I don't think Mrs. Carlisle is sick at all," he announced. "I think she's foxed."

"William!" Mrs. Black and I called out in unison. Mama started to cry. I got quickly to my feet to comfort Mama, but I did not realise that William was standing squarely on the hem of my gown. When I stood up, the basting threads around the bodice gave way. There I was, clad only in the bodice to my dress and my petticoat.

(I can hear you laughing. It's funny now; but believe that it was not funny this evening. At least to me. I admit that Uncle was highly diverted.)

Clarissa shrieked and held out her wrap to me. Mr. Rockingham sat down next to Mama, his eyes carefully averted from my undraped form. "Go away!" he hissed at Clarissa. She also started to cry. Mr. Rockingham put his arm around Mama's shoulders and murmured soothingly in her ear.

"Oh, my goodness," tittered Mrs. Black. Jeremy struggled to take off his very tight jacket.

"Liza, I'm sorry," William squealed, shocked into a high-pitched voice.

"Take my coat, my dear," Jeremy said officiously, peeling the right sleeve down his arm.

"No!" I said at last. I ran to the hall, my skirt hanging from the left side by a knot in the thread. I gave it a jerk and left the skirt there on the floor, while the company looked after me openmouthed.

My exit effectively put an end to the evening. The

Strathamsford party left shortly afterward. I was wearing a pink-flowered gown of Meg's—no, she has grown no taller nor no thinner since you left for war. The dress came considerably above my ankles, especially after I added a sash to gather in the ample waist; a generous six inches of my petticoat remained on display.

(You need not stretch your imagination, I'm sorry to say: Uncle grabbed his pocket sketch pad and muttered on the way home about capturing the exact shade of pink. No doubt you will receive the end result at Christmas.)

No one spoke from the time the Blacks' door closed behind us until we had left the carriage and entered our own front hallway. I had just pulled off my pelisse when Mr. Strickland and Rascal strolled out of the library.

"Giles!" exclaimed Mr. Rockingham happily. "You're back."

"Yes, about an hour ago," Mr. Strickland answered. "You're looking well, Dan." He turned to Mama. "Good evening, ma'am," he said with a bow. "I again trespass on your hospitality."

Mama pulled herself up tall and took a deep breath. "Welcome, sir," she answered in almost her normal voice. "I'm sorry we were not here to greet you. We dined with the Blacks."

Mr. Strickland looked me up and down from the six inches of petticoat to the absurdly puffed sleeves. "A costume party, I see," he commented. "Good evening, all."

It's astonishing how rapidly your heart will beat simply because someone sees you in a borrowed gown. "Good evening, sir," I said, willing myself to sound calm. The Whythes merely nodded as they started up the stairs to their chambers.

"Yes, my niece won first prize," Uncle remarked to our guest. "It's good to see you again, sir."

"It's good to be back, Mr. Martin," Mr. Strickland said.

"I wonder if I might have a few words with you after the rest of your family has retired?"

I gave Mr. Strickland a quizzical look which he answered with the merest twitch of his eyebrow. Nan, who had been waiting at the landing for the Whythes to climb the stairs, came down as Mama spoke. "I think Liza is as tired as I," she said. "Pray do not consider us in your plans."

"Our evening was not precisely restful," Mr. Rockingham explained to his friend. He released his right crutch to touch Mama's arm in farewell.

Nan and Mr. Strickland exchanged nods of acknowledgment before Nan stared in shock at me. "Liza, what happened?" she asked. "That's certainly not your gown."

I burst out laughing at her expression of disbelief and offered her the packet from which pieces of gold silk were escaping. "Tonight I learned that one must not move hastily when a large boy is standing on the hem of one's basted gown."

"I did this to you?" Nan asked in horror.

"You don't think pink flowers become me?" I teased, suddenly inexplicably giddy. I pirouetted so that Nan could get the full effect of the ridiculous sash which gathered the tent of dimity around my waist.

"She did this to you?" Mr. Strickland demanded, damping my high spirits. His eyes indicated that he was thinking I should learn how to find satisfactory servants.

Nan froze in her place and Uncle moved to put his arm around her shoulders. "I rather think William must bear the responsibility," he said, "since he was the boy standing on gold silk."

Mama was ashen. "No," she said quietly. "The fault is mine, for abusing the hospitality of our hosts."

"Nonsense!" I said perhaps too loudly. "I made a foolish move and now I present a foolish appearance. Surely justice is served." I went over to stand by Nan and Uncle since Mr. Rockingham still hovered protectively at Mama's side. "Perhaps we could talk tomorrow, sir," I looked a challenge at Mr. Strickland. "Since you speak with my uncle this evening."

"I would have suggested it if you had not," Mr. Strickland agreed. "Shall we walk before luncheon?"

"Yes," I said abruptly. He and Uncle disappeared into the library as the party dispersed in a flurry of good nights.

The hour is late as I write. I have soothed Mama and given Nan my unvarnished opinion of a certain gentleman. I only hope I have not dissipated my anger before my appointment to give him that same unvarnished opinion.

I haven't been paying close attention, but I'd swear that he and Uncle are still closeted in the library. I wonder if he brings encouraging news from the London gallery owner. Whatever I hear will be on its way to you as fast as a westbound ship can cross the Atlantic.

Need I mention how much I wish an eastbound ship would bring word for Strathamsford?

Truly I must retire to conserve my energy; tomorrow already promises to be as turbulent as today.

I trust your life is calm in comparison to that of your loving

Elizabeth

Conversation revised

Elizabeth: Tonight I learned that one must not move hastily when a large boy is standing on the hem of one's basted gown.

Mr. Strickland: I think instead you should learn how to find satisfactory servants.

E: My servants are perfectly satisfactory. I had rather learn how to find satisfactory houseguests.

Mr. S: You didn't find us, exactly. It would be more precise to say that Dan Rockingham dropped in.

E: You're right. I would never dream of choosing you. Or, if I did, would call it a nightmare.

Please disregard the above. It is worthy neither of me nor of my opponent.

Elizabeth: Perhaps we could talk tomorrow.

Mr. Strickland: Shall we walk before luncheon?

E: Yes, leaving the house would be wise. I may raise my voice.

Mr. S: Why do you not raise your voice to someone who has earned it?

E: But I do, sir.

Good night.
E.

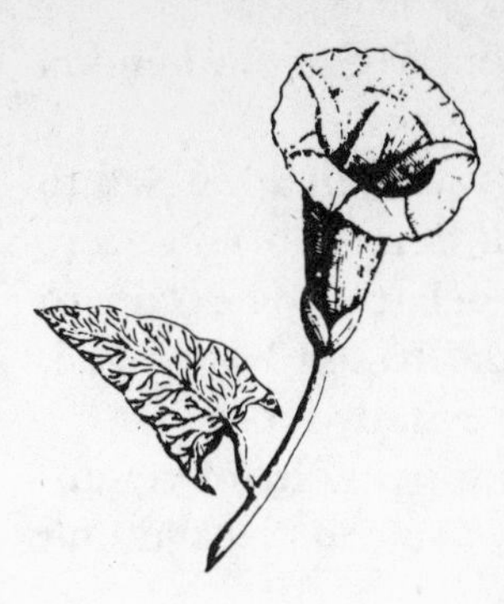

Friday afternoon, 22 October, 1813

Dearest Brother,

Please forgive me for not beginning this letter, as Mama taught us to do, with an enquiry about your activities and state of health. My mind is filled only with my own concerns. I'm ashamed to admit it. But I am certain that if you were here—and how I wish you were—you would understand.

Mama insisted on coming down early this morning although she was deathly pale; everyone apologised to everyone else and agreed that something must have been amiss in the phases of the moon. Cousin Clarissa and Aunt Charlotte had obviously had a long and very cozy chat: Clarissa seemed to have switched the glare of her attention back to Mr. Strickland. (Is it too catty of me to suggest that Mr. Rockingham looked relieved?)

Mr. Strickland has indeed arranged for a London showing of Uncle's work. Uncle is quietly euphoric; I will give you details as I learn them.

My antagonist and I were just leaving with a virtual absence of chitchat for our scheduled walk, when William Black appeared at the front door with a whole armload of flowers. He must have scooped up every chrysanthemum in the county.

Mr. Strickland burst out laughing as I called for Nan to help me relieve William of his burden. "So you were indeed the culprit in last night's debacle," he said to William. "You have improved on the lesson I gave you: when dealing with women, more is usually more."

"In this case," I remonstrated, smiling in spite of myself, "too much is too much. William, you needn't have. But thank you; they're lovely."

"I'm sorry, Liza; really I am," William said eagerly. "I didn't mean to, honest."

"Of course you didn't," I said. "Let's agree to blame the threadmaker."

"Sometime you must tell me exactly what happened last night," Mr. Strickland said to me. There was a smile in his eyes.

"I expect to," I replied in what I hoped was a daunting tone. "That's why we arranged this walk."

"Oh, you're going for a walk?" asked William excitedly. "I'll come with you. Can we go toward . . . ?"

"William, go home," ordered Mr. Strickland. "Miss Carlisle and I hope to have a peaceful stroll, and it seems you bring disaster."

I doubted that our conference would prove tranquil, but I concurred with his wish for privacy. "Another day, William," I assured him. "The flowers will help both my mother and me forget last evening. Thank you again."

We bid our respective farewells; as William bounded off toward the parsonage, Mr. Strickland and I headed down the back lane toward the woodlot.

"You will feel quite the belle of the village," Mr. Strickland mused aloud when we had left Strathamsford behind. "I've brought a present for you too."

"I wish you would not try to flatter me with kind words

and gifts as well," I reproved him. "I am determined to be angry with you."

Mr. Strickland seemed genuinely surprised. "You are?" he asked. "I didn't think you were in earnest."

"Truly I am," I repeated. "I am angered every time you disparage Nan Andrews, and you did it again last night."

"I said nothing," he protested.

"You were thinking it," I insisted foolishly.

There was a pause. "You must admit she seems incompetent," he remarked. "Is that why you wished to speak to me?"

I stopped in the path and stamped my foot. "Nan is not incompetent!" I declared. "She sometimes seems giddy, but in fact she is at least as able as I."

"Try to be rational, Liza," Mr. Strickland said. "We are discussing your maid. You are blinded by your affection for her, which is to your credit."

"This conversation is not to yours, sir," I repaid his overfamiliar use of my nickname with a gratuitous insult. "You need never fear that I will be blinded by my affection for *you*."

"You have a quick temper, my dear," Mr. Strickland corrected me gently, "and sometimes say things you do not mean."

I took a deep breath so that I could tell him just how fervently I mean the things I say, but he took my arm and shushed me to silence. "Let's just walk for a time, and when you're more in charity with me I'll give you your present," he said.

"I don't want a present," it shames me to report I replied.

"You might," he said, drawing my arm through his and starting on down the lane. "There's your temper again."

I had no choice but to follow along, and if the truth be told I was soothed by the touch of his arm. I even granted him perception about my character: I am quick to anger, and all too often I say things I don't mean.

(You may sense a certain reluctance, dear Brother, to remember the more tender nuances of my story: the reason will be evident before you have finished this letter.)

Mr. Strickland and I walked for almost a quarter of an hour before either of us spoke. Even Rascal, who had of course accompanied us, ambled quietly along. Finally Mr. Strickland put his left hand over mine resting on his arm.

"Are you feeling more kindly toward me now?" he asked, looking down at me with a smile.

"I am, yes," I answered, "but the cause may be the brilliant morning rather than a mellowing of my opinions." I paused. "We have not yet come to any understanding, you know."

"I hope we may," he said with such sincerity that I stopped to study him questioningly.

He took his hand from mine, reached into the pocket of his coat, and pulled out the largest sapphire I have ever seen. I stood speechless, gazing into the blue infinity in his palm.

"Of course a diamond is more versatile," he said to my stunned ears. "But this is quite a good stone." He turned the jewel in his hand and I saw that it was set in a ring. I'm afraid my mouth dropped open.

"Will you do me the honour, Miss Carlisle, of becoming my wife?" Mr. Strickland asked. The sun glinted off the sapphire to hurt my eyes, so I looked up wordlessly at my companion.

"I'd rather squabble with you than live peaceably with anyone else," he said with the irresistible smile I believe I have mentioned before.

At last I was startled into speech. "You have taken me completely by surprise, sir," I admitted, stalling for time while I cast about for a way to reply.

"I think, under the circumstances, that you might call

me Giles," he corrected. He tried to draw me closer, but I pulled away.

"You have not yet had my answer," I said. "I am convinced we would not suit."

It was Mr. Strickland's turn to look startled. "Surely we should suit very well," he protested. "Our thoughts often run on parallel tracks."

"Perhaps so," I agreed, "but more often they run on perpendicular ones. And collision is the result."

Mr. Strickland closed his fingers over the brilliant ring and I felt as if the sun had gone behind a cloud, although it was shining as brightly as before. "Minor disagreements can lend spice to life," he commented.

"Yes," I said. "But major ones may spoil it."

"You believe we have major disagreements," he said. It was a statement, not a question.

"And yet you are convinced we do not," I said. "That's a major disagreement in itself."

Mr. Strickland replaced the ring in the pocket of his jacket. "Have we, by any chance, returned to a discussion of servants?" he asked, exasperated.

"Yes," I said without embellishment.

"You seem overmuch concerned about your maid," he insisted. "Is there something I don't know about Nan Andrews?"

"There certainly is," I answered. "A person need not be on your social level to deserve your respect. You deny her basic consideration."

"Surely I have not mistreated your maid," Mr. Strickland protested. "What did I do that you resent so bitterly?"

"It's your attitude, your assumption that she has no more complexities of feeling than Rascal here," I explained, gaining steam. "You treat servants as if they were slow-witted children."

"Dan Rockingham does not seem to feel that I misuse him," he objected.

"No doubt you are blinded by your affection for him," I repeated spitefully. The ridiculousness of our conversation hit me suddenly and I giggled. "This must be a singular proposal of marriage," I said without thinking. "My other offer was far different."

"Your other offer?" Mr. Strickland asked. "So the vicar's son did come up to scratch." He considered my revelation. "Why did you refuse him?"

"Pray forget I mentioned it, sir," I pleaded. "It was indiscreet. As you know, I do not choose to wed."

"I don't know why you rejected Mr. Black, but I consider your reasons for refusing me to be capricious," Mr. Strickland pronounced. "We will speak of this later."

"I beg you to consider the matter closed," I said. "I am greatly complimented by your offer of marriage, but I cannot accept it."

"Then you will oblige me by thinking no more about it," Mr. Strickland said. He took my arm once again and steered me around so that we were heading back toward Strathamsford. "Your uncle is pleased, I believe," he said, "that his paintings are to be shown in London."

"Oh, yes," I said. I had no need to feign an enthusiasm which may have been enhanced by his change of subject. "You were very kind to arrange it for him."

"Please do not consider it a courtesy," Mr. Strickland insisted. "Your uncle's work deserves a wider audience than it can reach in the country."

"What exactly did the gallery owner say about my uncle's paintings?" I asked.

"He said they have 'integrity,' " he answered solemnly.

"Does that mean Uncle can draw an iris recognisable as an iris?" I asked. I couldn't help smiling.

Mr. Strickland returned my smile. "If your uncle is to travel in artistic circles, you must learn the artistic code words," he said; he spoke amusingly of harmony and texture, scale and intensity all the way home.

You can imagine that I was not as calm as I appeared at luncheon. In spite of his request that I forget it, my astonishing conversation with Mr. Strickland kept replaying in my head. Thus I was able to ignore Clarissa's inane chatter, which was directed mainly at the subject of my thoughts. By the end of the meal I became aware that she was attempting to engage him for the afternoon.

"And since you forgot to purchase my slippers in London," Clarissa trilled, "I think you must take me driving this afternoon."

"I would be delighted to," Mr. Strickland said, acting delighted, "if Mrs. Carlisle can spare a carriage. Perhaps we could head toward the abbey I've heard so much about."

Because I was being careful not to look at the speaker, I caught the glance which passed between Mama and Mr. Rockingham. "Of course you may take a carriage," Mama offered. "Mr. Rockingham and I plan a quiet afternoon, since he went out last evening."

Mr. Rockingham smiled warmly at Mama; and Aunt Charlotte beamed at her daughter. "That will be . . ." Aunt Charlotte said happily as the party broke up.

I'll admit I felt a little left out, especially since I truly felt the need of company. I went back to the kitchen to see if Nan had helped with luncheon, but Cook reminded me that she is watching Missy and Thomas this afternoon while their parents go to market.

I checked the studio to see if Uncle would be glad of a guest. He was there all right, completely surrounded by several circles of sketches and paintings.

"What on earth are you doing?" I asked from the door. I didn't dare go in; I might have stepped on a work of art.

"Hello, Liza," Uncle said. "Would you help me choose what to send to London? I've gotten everything out—"

"I can see that," I interrupted. "I had no idea you had done so many."

"Nor had I," Uncle agreed. "And some of them I'm ashamed to claim. But several I've decided I'm quite proud of."

I inched into the studio and craned my neck for a better view. "I'd forgotten the still life with Mama's blue vase. And the barns in springtime." I leaned forward until I almost lost my balance. "But what is that mishmash over the corner? I can't place it."

Uncle chuckled. "Remember when I decided to try oil pigments? That muddle explains why I have continued with watercolour."

"How many does the gallery want?" I asked.

"I won't know until I've talked to the owner," Uncle answered. "I expect to go to the city immediately with several more samples of my work." With a tape rule, he measured both sides of the still life with blue vase and made notations on the pad beside him. "I'm ready now, I think, to make crates for these. Will you come with me to the workshed?"

"Why, how soon do you leave?" I asked. "Not tomorrow?"

"Tomorrow early," Uncle confirmed, but his mind was obviously on his quandry. "I can't decide between the landscape and the abbey," he said. He looked at me questioningly.

"Why do you not take both?" I suggested. "And if you choose the sketch of Mama in the garden, you'll have someone to talk to."

Uncle nodded; he seemed pleased to concur. "I'll make a bigger crate," he said, gathering up his notes and his measure. "Shall we go?"

"You don't need me," I said. "Maybe I'll write a letter to my brother."

Uncle stopped in the doorway to gaze at the sketch of Mama I had pointed out. "Is Liza all right, do you think?" he asked Mama's image. "She does not seem quite happy."

"Yes," I answered. "Yes, I'm fine."

But somehow I'm not sure that I am.

Since everyone else at Strathamsford is busy, I've spent the afternoon with you. Surely you know that if you were here, you would be at the other end of my list.

Nan has come in from the south farm and reports seeing Cousin Clarissa and Mr. Strickland drive by, merry as grigs. They deserve each other.

No, I take that back. It's not kind, however true it may be.

You see: I need you here to show me the humour in all this. For some reason I feel like crying.

Love from
your silly
Elizabeth

Conversation revised

Elizabeth: I am determined to be angry with you.
Mr. Strickland: But I've brought you a present.
E: Do you follow your own teaching, sir? More is more?
Mr. S: You must decide that for yourself. Will you wear this engagement ring?
E: No, no, no, no, no.
Mr. S: The lady doth protest too much, methinks.

You can see I am still flustered beyond sense. And I do not look forward to this evening, which will no doubt be reported by

E.

Saturday morning, 23 October, 1813

Dearest Brother,

The sky has just become light enough for me to see the page on which I write. I was restless all the night—I believe I heard the hall clock chime every hour but two o'clock. Rather than toss any more, I took pen and paper as the darkness faded, cautioned Rascal to be quiet, woke and saddled Lilac, and rode out to the abbey. I am hoping that I will absorb enough of its serenity to tell you calmly about last evening, which was far from calm.

Apparently Cousin Clarissa and Mr. Strickland had a fine time on their drive; both were in high spirits when we assembled before dinner. (You will note that I am no longer the recipient of Clarissa's confidences.) Mr. Strickland was wearing a sapphire in his cravat which was almost as large as the one he offered to me in the afternoon. I realised with a start that his stickpin was designed as a companion-piece to the ring. Clarissa's eyes bugged out at the sight of it.

She didn't say anything, though, until after dinner when we had adjourned to the drawing room. Then she was unable to restrain herself any longer. "Your sapphire is breathtaking, Mr. Strickland," she cooed. "Did you bring it from India?"

"Yes, I did," he answered. "The setting was new last week. Do you like it?"

"It's the biggest stone I've ever seen," Clarissa gushed. "Do you have many jewels so large?" She looked up at him from under her eyelashes.

"Just one sapphire that is larger," Mr. Strickland said. He turned to me as he spoke and I looked away after only an instant. I could feel his gaze as Uncle jumped to my rescue.

"Would you mind terribly, my dear," he said to Mama, "if I spent the evening in the workshed? I must finish crating the samples for the gallery."

"I'm sure the others will excuse you," Mama answered. She looked around at the group for agreement. "How shall we spend the evening? Liza, have you any suggestion?"

I fear I was looking at her stupidly when Cousin Clarissa made her own proposal. "Oh, do let's play whist," she said vivaciously. "I feel very lucky tonight."

"That sounds like a challenge to me," Mr. Strickland retorted. "What do you say, Dan?"

"Mrs. Carlisle and I were going to plan a new kitchen garden," Mr. Rockingham demurred. "Perhaps Mrs. Whythe would take a hand."

"Oh, no," said Aunt Charlotte quickly. "I must finish . . ." She gestured vaguely toward her sewing bag.

"Please play," Mama said quietly. "We can plan the garden tomorrow."

"That settles it," announced Mr. Strickland. "Dan and I hereby challenge you (he looked provocatively at Cousin Clarissa)—and your cousin, of course—to a game of whist." I could have screamed. "Name your stakes," he drawled at Clarissa.

"No stakes," I said grimly.

"House rules," Mr. Rockingham added. "You remember, Giles."

"Oh, yes," Mr. Strickland said. "But surely Mrs. Carlisle could have no objection to a small side bet between two players, so long as no money is involved." He turned to Mama with a questioning smile which was supposed to have great charm.

"Why, no, I guess not," Mama agreed. She looked at me for confirmation and I managed to give her a slight nod.

"But what shall we play for, sir?" Clarissa asked coyly. She gazed up through her eyelashes and I felt a little queasy.

"Winner names the stakes," declared Mr. Strickland. He gave Clarissa what I would have to describe as a leer.

So we played whist. As the evening progressed, my uneasiness was transformed into fury: you would not believe the blatant flirtation which Mr. Rockingham and I had perforce to witness. Mama was spared because of Aunt Charlotte's chatter; when there was a lull in their conversation, there always seemed to be a lull in talk at the card table as well. It pains me to admit that the score was extremely one-sided. Clarissa never could play cards.

My temper, alas, was near to the boiling point when Mr. Strickland said gravely to Clarissa, "Is it fair, do you think, to measure the seriousness of your forfeit by the size of your loss?"

Clarissa giggled. "Oh, I pray you, sir, be merciful," she tittered. "Come, Liza, we must contrive to win this round."

"Your cousin cannot save you from defeat now," Mr. Strickland gloated over my silence. "But perhaps I can assess a penalty which you will enjoy as much as I." He gazed at Clarissa intently and she had the grace to blush.

All of a sudden I could not stand the drawing room another instant. "I find I have the headache," I said to Mr. Rockingham. "Could we finish the game tomorrow?"

"I'm so sorry, Miss Carlisle," Mr. Rockingham said sympathetically. "Perhaps your mother has a remedy." He looked to Mama, but she had not heard.

"Truly, I think all I need is a quick word with Mr. Strickland in the library before I take myself off to bed," I said, smiling far more kindly than I wished to.

Mr. Strickland smiled back just as kindly and no doubt just as sincerely. "Perhaps our talk, like the game, should wait until tomorrow," he suggested.

"No," I said firmly. "I will feel better for speaking with you tonight."

I made my good nights, as did Mr. Strickland; and we walked silently to the library. He stepped back to let me precede him through the door, but I waited inside the room to shut it behind him.

"This is to be a closed-door discussion?" he asked, amused.

"Indeed it is," I sputtered, letting my anger show at last. "You are a contemptible man."

"I thought we established that fact earlier today," Mr. Strickland commented. "It surely has not just occurred to you."

Well, Brother, you remember what suspecting I am being toyed with does to my temper. It did so again. I exploded. "How you treat me is one thing," I said furiously. "I know what you are and do not consider you seriously. But my cousin is more easily impressed."

Mr. Strickland tried to interrupt but I hurtled on. "You flirted outrageously with her all evening long simply to get your revenge on me, and the poor woman is without doubt upstairs this very minute planning her trousseau. It's not fair," I finished decisively. I stood, feet apart, hands on hips, daring my adversary to contradict me.

But he simply stared at me. He just stood there.

Finally I said, "Well?"

"Are you quite done?" Mr. Strickland asked.

"Yes," I said.

"It's my turn?" he asked.

"Yes," I said again, looking daggers at him. "What have you to say for yourself?"

"First of all," he began, "your cousin Clarissa has no need of your protection." I dropped my hands from my hips; it was not at all what I expected him to say. "She is a calculating young woman," he went on, "who can enjoy a flirtation for what it is. And even if she has hopes of me at the moment, her feelings do not begin to be engaged."

Two can play his game. I simply looked at him.

"Surely you cannot in honesty tell me," Mr. Strickland asserted, "that you think Clarissa cares more for me than for the wedding ring I could give her?"

"I *can* tell you in all honesty that I believe you would not make my cousin happy," I responded.

"You're right, of course," he agreed. "Any more than that pompous parson's son would bring you joy."

I took a deep breath and walked over to sit on the divan under the window. "It's silly to rip up at each other," I said. "I ask simply that you not use my cousin as a means of exasperating me."

"So you confess you were exasperated?" Mr. Strickland asked. This time he used his charming smile on me.

"Clarissa is too ambitious," I said after a moment's thought. "Maybe you'd do better to court someone just out of the schoolroom." I warmed to my subject. "A girl who would be staggered by the jewels and easily moulded to the wife you want."

"You go too far, Liza," he said, angry himself at last. "If I wish a conformable wife, I need not mould her myself. Her mother is trying to do that."

"Are you referring to your hostess, sir?" I asked grimly.

"Of course," Mr. Strickland agreed. "But that in itself is not a criticism. I have no quarrel with her aim, my dear; but I regret her method."

"And how do you perceive her method, sir?" I asked. I

stood to tap my foot, which you—if not he—would know for a bad sign.

"Whenever anything happens to upset her, she reaches for her decanter," he charged. "It looks like blackmail to me."

I know the colour drained out of my face. "You have now insulted my mother, my maid, my cousin, and my neighbour," I said, making a conscious effort to keep my voice down. "I feel slighted. Surely you have an insult left for me."

Mr. Strickland took two steps to close the space between us. He reached out to hold my arms to my sides as if he was going to shake me. Instead he pulled me against him and kissed me—hard.

At first I was too stunned to react. His kiss was completely different from Jeremy's: I felt it not only on my lips but all the way to my toes. Then he took his hands from my shoulders to embrace me tightly. Somehow my arms were around his neck and I decided that lovemaking is not overrated after all.

Then Rascal scratched at the door, and my euphoria evaporated. I remembered that this man was trying to insult me, not to secure my affections. I broke free from his arms, stepped back, and slapped him.

Mr. Strickland simply stood there. He stared into my eyes for an endless moment as if he wished to read my thoughts. Then without saying a single word, he turned on his heel and left the room, closing the door behind him. But a large dog managed to slip into the library.

I sank onto the divan, my mind a complete blank. Since I didn't know what to think, my head refused to work at all. Rascal came over to lick my hand; I'm sure your animal was alarmed at my trance.

"It's all right, Rascal," I reassured him, scratching between his silky ears.

Rascal flopped down beside me, his head on my foot.

And he has stuck right by my side since. The sun is high now at the abbey, and I've thrown off the heavy cape I put on at dawn. We'll go back to Strathamsford by way of the post office, so this letter gets mailed before second thoughts consign it to the fire.

You need not wade through a foolish conversation. Instead my mind is full of questions:

1. Can I admit that he is right about Clarissa?
2. Is it possible that Mama's problem has become an unconscious form of blackmail?
3. Where will I find another man whose kiss is as intoxicating as Giles Strickland's?
4. Why isn't my brother here to advise his confused

Elizabeth

Saturday, 23 October, 1813
En route to Southampton

Uncle dear,

(I usually begin my letters "Dearest Brother." It seems strange to be writing to my uncle instead.)

You left for London just an hour before we got word from Southampton that my brother has arrived there on a hospital ship: he was injured in the same battle at Baltimore in which General Ross was killed. The communiqué we received gave no details about his condition, but I am dismayed that the message was not written in his own hand. Of course I will send you word as soon as I have seen him.

I had gone to the abbey just after dawn to write to my brother, which was why I was not at home to bid you farewell. When I stopped by the post office to mail the letter—I wonder if he will ever see it now—Mr. Gribbs told me that he had sent a boy to Strathamsford with a message from the War Office.

I raced home at a dead gallop—poor Lilac did not understand why we were in such a hurry—to find Strathamsford, as you could guess, in an uproar.

Apparently Nan had answered the door to the boy, and

then delivered the message to Mama. Mama read the letter, handed it to Nan, and collapsed into a fit of sobbing. I got my information from Mr. Rockingham, who came to Mama's aid as quickly as crutches would allow him.

Mr. Rockingham poured Mama a glass of brandy (and, I gather, another and another) so that by the time I arrived Mama was two sheets to the wind, still sobbing uncontrollably.

"Where's Nan?" I asked Mr. Rockingham as he handed Mama a fresh handkerchief; he held her within the circle of his arm.

"She went to Southampton," he said. "I assumed you knew."

All of a sudden I understood: Nan's lack of interest in other men, her endless letter-writing. She's been in love all along with my brother! Did you know? I feel very foolish to have been so oblivious.

"I'm shamefaced to say I did not," I answered Mr. Rockingham. "Did she leave me no word?"

"She left a note with your mother," he said. He leaned across Mama to search between the cushions on the sofa. "I don't see it now. "Do you know what happened to Nan's message, Helen?" he asked Mama.

"My poor son," Mama looked up at me befuddled. "Will you go to him, Liza? I'm too ill."

"Of course, Mama," I said. "I'll write as soon as I've seen him." Mr. Rockingham and I exchanged a look which promised concern and care on both sides.

Trying to consider half a dozen problems at once, I hurried to my bedchamber and threw a change of clothes into the first bag I pulled from the floor of the clothespress. My immediate concern was finding someone to accompany me to Southampton—we needed to leave at once to arrive by nightfall and chaperone Nan properly.

Alas, the man whose escort would have been most welcome cared a fig for neither Nan's reputation nor a woman who abused him not only verbally but physically as well. (Some day, dear Uncle, I'll explain.)

By the time I dropped my bag downstairs and hastened to the kitchen—it was difficult to put up a food basket when I have no idea what is wrong with my brother—I had decided to enlist Jeremy Black. Jem took a note: "Please, Jeremy," I scrawled, "Come with me to Southampton. My brother is wounded and Nan has gone to him. I would be grateful for your company."

Jem left for the vicarage and my mind raced ahead of him. We would have to take a carriage: not only was Lilac exhausted but you know that if we rode, Rascal would howl for hours. Mama could never bear it.

I packed basket and bag in the landau; I was adding blankets and clothing for my brother when Jem returned with Jeremy's answer.

"I will be pleased to offer you my protection," he wrote, "but I cannot possibly leave until Monday. Surely your maid will inform you if your brother's need of you is immediate. I will call tomorrow to arrange our travel."

I crumpled his note and tossed it to the ground. Jem picked the note up and put it back in my hand before he reached out to take part of my burden. I handed him a quilt and decided that I would rather travel with a groom than ask such a favour of the man with whom—I'm sorry to admit it, Uncle—I quarrelled last night.

As if my thought conjured him up, Mr. Strickland rode into the stableyard. "Is something wrong?" he asked, off his horse in an instant. "Where are you going?"

"My brother is wounded," I explained as I stacked the last bundle into the landau. "Nan has already left for Southampton, where he is, and I must join her there."

"Let me go with you," he said at once. "We can be on the road in five minutes."

"But—" I hesitated.

"What is it?" he asked.

"I owe you an apology for last night," I began.

Mr. Strickland cut me off. "We'll talk later, Lily," he said. I blinked at his use of my old nickname. "I'll be right back," he called over his shoulder, striding toward the house. "Harness the pair, Jem."

And so we have set off for Southampton. Nan, of course, took the stage. We would have caught up with her before this, except that Mr. Strickland suggested he try to arrange a special license when we stopped for lunch. Then Nan and my brother can marry immediately if they wish, and Nan will face no more whispers than necessary when she becomes mistress of Strathamsford.

Mr. Strickland is sealing his letters, so I must close. I think there is no reason now for you to disrupt your business in London. I shall send a further message as soon as I have seen my brother. He will join me, I know, in hoping that you are as pleased with the gallery as they are with your work.

Be careful! One invalid is all we can manage to care for, I fear. And write soon to

Elizabeth

Sunday morning, 24 October, 1813
At Southampton

Dearest Mama,

My brother will regain his health. That is the news you wish to hear, I know, and I am thrilled to be able to tell it. Although he must remain here for some weeks, he appears to be gaining strength simply from being again on British soil. I hope we may soon have him home at Strathamsford.

His wound is a serious one below his right elbow. The doctor in America believed his life in danger unless his lower arm was amputated, but my brother flatly refused the surgery. His mind, I am told, was wandering when Nan arrived late yesterday afternoon, but her presence was so therapeutic that he came to himself and slept calmly last night for several hours. Nan sat with him until dawn, when I insisted that she take some rest. I write at the table beside his bed. My brother has just awakened: when I told him who was to receive my report he whispered the word "love."

Which brings me to my other news: Nan and my brother are married! Did you know? I swear I did not. My brother got his own special license before he took his commission and demanded that Nan become his wife. He may have been wise: since she had these months to become accustomed to the idea, Nan has taken over here as if she had given orders all her life. Though I confess that I did not know what to think when Mr. Strickland and I arrived at the infirmary to be told that Mrs. Carlisle was sitting with her husband.

But let me back up to tell you of our trip. Mr. Strickland offered to bring me to Southampton as soon as he learned of my brother's arrival here. As you know, I have not always enjoyed Mr. Strickland's company, and rarely less so than the night before we came to Southampton. So I was pleasantly surprised to find him all practical compassion on our journey.

It was, for instance, his idea that we arrange for a special license to be delivered in Southampton. When we stopped for luncheon he sent directions to London while I wrote to Uncle there. I trust Uncle will not cut short his business; when you write to him, please urge him to stay as long as needs be to complete it.

As we neared Southampton, I confess I was apprehensive, both about my brother's condition and about Nan's flight to him.

"Why do you suppose Nan left so suddenly?" I asked my companion finally. "Does she know something more than we know?"

"She left you a note, did she not?" Mr. Strickland answered.

"But I did not see it," I fretted. "Surely she had no more details than we."

"You'll know within the hour," Mr. Strickland soothed me.

Of course he was right. And I found out much more than I expected to. Did you find the note, Mama? And did you read it? If so, the fact of my brother's marriage is surely not news to you. I have not had a chance to ask Nan about her note; I'm sure her departure yesterday from Strathamsford seems a lifetime ago.

Nan has already made my brother as comfortable as it is possible for him to be. Mr. Strickland and I will look this afternoon for a house to take when my brother may be moved. My escort has sent to London for a doctor about whom he has had fine reports, but truly I think our patient is well past the worst. His contentment in Nan's company is patently obvious, and he felt well enough last evening to notice the new way I wear my hair. I did not even mind that he does not approve it.

Mr. Strickland and I have yet to discuss our journey back to Strathamsford. I hope he will agree to remain here until my brother is settled outside hospital. I shall write again if we are not to be home within the week.

Please do not feel that you must rush to Southampton. When Mr. Strickland's doctor has seen our patient and given us an idea how soon he may be moved, we can make more definite plans. I'll let you know as soon as we hear from London.

And please excuse this disjointed letter. I got little sleep last night—and if truth be told, the night before as well—so my mind is not much swifter than my brother's. Nan has just come in, so I will close and go to my own bed. If only I could look so radiant after a few hours rest. But of course rest does not account for her bloom. If that is love, perhaps I should try some.

You see, I am giddy with exhaustion. Do not take seriously

your affectionate
Elizabeth

Monday evening, 25 October, 1813
At Southampton

Uncle dear,

You would not believe the change in my brother in just the past twenty-four hours! He is so much better that he is beginning to eat a little solid food. I had thrown some dishes from the kitchen at Strathamsford into a basket before I left home, and he actually asked if I had brought any of Mama's trifle.

His arm improves so rapidly that there is no question now of amputation. Mr. Strickland has sent for a doctor from London, but we are so heartened today that Mr. Strickland and I will not wait to see him.

Did Mama write to you that Nan and my brother were married in the spring? I am surprised how easily I have become accustomed to the idea: probably because I have loved them both all my life, it seems natural for them to love each other.

This afternoon Mr. Strickland and I found a tiny house to let, convenient both to the hospital and to the shops. Nan moves in tomorrow, and we hope it will soon receive our patient, who already is eager to be away from the ward of wounded men.

“It’s so small,” I said to Mr. Strickland as we walked back to the hospital from the estate agent’s. “Do you think we can manage?”

“Nan—Mrs. Carlisle—seems to be managing perfectly well,” he answered. “She won’t need more than two bedchambers unless the whole family insists on playing nurse.”

“She does, doesn’t she?” I agreed, smiling up at him. (Have I told you, Uncle, that Mr. Strickland and I have quarrelled about the treatment of servants? At least—no matter what his feelings—he can be counted on in an emergency.)

“Won’t your mother wish to come to Southampton?” Mr. Strickland asked. “Surely she must see her son’s condition for herself.”

“Of course,” I said, “and there will hardly be room for us all on High Street.”

“Perhaps you and I should return to Strathamsford,” he suggested. “Dan Rockingham must be able to travel now at least as far as London. Then we should be out of your way.”

For some reason my heart dropped. “You’ve hardly been in our way,” I protested. “I could not have come to Southampton nor Mama stayed at home without you and your friend.”

Mr. Strickland did not speak for several endless seconds. Then he put his hand under my elbow so that we were walking quite close together. “I have another suggestion,” he said. He looked down at me. “There’s a special license in my pocket.”

I stopped dead on the sidewalk and turned wordlessly to face him. “Since your brother has no need of it, I thought we might use it,” he went on. He flashed me a smile that crumpled my heart where it lay.

I was spared making answer when Nan called out to us from across the street. “Were you successful?” she asked, once greetings had been exchanged. "Did you find a place?"

"Yes, we have taken a house," I said, careful not to look at Mr. Strickland. "And I hope it will do. The rooms are not big, but it's very near."

"I'm so glad," Nan said, and moved on to her next problem. "Have you seen a chemist's shop? My husband needs a razor and (she consulted a list in her hand) a mug with soap and a brush so that I can shave him." She hurried on to cover her blush. "Do you think we might have light meals sent over from the inn? The hospital's food is most unappetizing."

"Of course," I said; "I should have thought of it."

"I noticed a chemist just around the corner," Mr. Strickland answered to Nan's first question. "May we walk along with you? Perhaps I could help choose your purchases."

"Oh, would you, sir?" Nan asked gratefully. "I'm completely at sea."

We turned to retrace our steps, Nan between Mr. Strickland and me. "We were just discussing whether or not he and I should stay in Southampton," I said to Nan. Mr. Strickland seemed about to speak, but I continued. "None of us packed more than the barest necessities. If he and I go home, we can send your things and whatever my brother needs." I paused to take a breath. "Maybe Mama will come too. And the tiny house will not accommodate us all."

Nan, whose eyes had been on her feet, looked up in apprehension. "Will she mind, Liza?" she asked. "About Edward and me? I've worried a great deal about it."

"Of course not," I said instantly. "Even if she was not already fond of you, she will see that having you beside him is better medicine than anything my brother's doctors could prescribe." I put my arm around her shoulders to give her a quick hug. "Nan!" I exclaimed as a thought struck me. "We're sisters now."

Nan laughed. "Does that mean you will leave me your shawl?" she asked. "I came away without one."

"Marriage does not appear to have improved your organisation," I commented, pretending to be serious.

Mr. Strickland looked at me reprovingly. "If I had said that, there would be fireworks," he charged.

"She's not *your* sister," I protested. Nan and I giggled as the three of us entered the chemist's shop.

We were busy the rest of the day making arrangements. Since only one person at a time may sit with my brother, we managed in rotation. I remained at the hospital while Nan and Mr. Strickland engaged a housekeeper to move tomorrow to the tiny house with Mrs. Carlisle. (Her new name still sounds strange on my tongue. But Nan acts as if she has been called Mrs. Carlisle always.)

Then Mr. Strickland stayed with my brother while Nan and I assembled lists of items to be sent from Strathamsford to Southampton: furnishings and kitchenware to make the house more comfortable, clothes for both my brother and Nan, books, Nan's needlework. If they are to stay there any length of time, no doubt even Rascal will make the trip.

So Mr. Strickland and I leave in the morning for Strathamsford. Nan, who started life as the housekeeper's daughter, moves into a rented house with a housekeeper of her own. And my brother, I pray, recovers his strength even more quickly than the doctors hope he will.

I am eager to hear—last mentioned does not mean least thought of—about your adventures in London. When will the gallery hang your paintings? Do they plan a one-man show? You needn't sell the pictures that belong at Strathamsford surely. You stand warned: if all exhibits must be offered for sale, my birthday daffodils do not leave the house.

Please write to me—or to Mama. Or better yet to my

brother. He is feeling well enough to ask questions about his family, and he, too, is eager to hear about your trip.

Love from
Elizabeth

Conversation revised

Mr. Strickland: Dan Rockingham and I should get out of your way.
Elizabeth: Is that what you wish?
Mr. S: No, I would prefer to make use of the special license in my pocket. If I ask you again to marry me, might I receive a different answer?
E: You do not tempt me this time with a sapphire which would never fit inside a glove.
Mr. S: I had not thought of that. I suppose it wouldn't. But is that a reason to refuse me a second time?
E: Actually I've been thinking that your outrageous stone might become my left hand.
Mr. S: I'm supposed to kiss you now. Will you slap me again?
E: Will you bribe me with jewels?
Mr. S: You must kiss me to find out, my love.
E: Then so must you.
(They kiss.)

Oh, Uncle. When I let my imagination run wild, I can compose quite a nice love scene. I wonder what Mr. Strickland would think of it. And I wonder what comes next. You will receive an early report from

your daydreaming
E.

Wednesday morning, 27 October, 1813

Dearest Brother and Sister,

Everything at Strathamsford is at joyous sixes and sevens. If only you both were here to share in the blissful chaos, life would seem perfect. Although of course if you both were here, we would be far less chaotic.

Mama, as you can guess, is ecstatic at the news that you, my brother, may regain full use of your arm. She sings as she bustles around pulling this and that from its storage place to put on the mountain of items destined for Southampton. So far she has gathered enough things to fill your tiny house two times over, and she is far from finished.

(Part of the problem lies in her concurrent happiness in learning of your marriage. "It's their first home," she says; "they will want to remember something lovely on the walls." Or "How can Nan possibly set up housekeeping without a curtain stretcher?" Do you see the extent of our difficulty? I'll do my best to see that it does not become *your* difficulty.)

And Uncle has written from London that Mr. Strickland's friend, the gallery owner—I've forgotten his name—is so taken with Uncle's paintings that he wishes to open the exhibit before Christmas. Imagine: our very own Uncle hobnobbing with the Royal Academy! Perhaps he will give you a picture for a bride's gift, and you will indeed have something lovely on the walls of your first home.

At Uncle's request, Mr. Rockingham is trying to make an inventory of the paintings here. He is ensconced in the studio; since Mama does not trust Mr. Strickland and me to help him find the works scattered through the house, she darts from room to room mixing your requests with my uncle's. (If you receive a crate of paintings, please readdress it to London.)

And to complete the upheaval, Cousin Clarissa and Aunt Charlotte are packing up to leave before luncheon. No, I've decided that Strathamsford is not nearly restful enough for an invalid. You are much better off in Southampton, dear Brother.

I need not tell you that I am feeling giddy today. But I do need to tell you two more pieces of news, and I shall try to restrain my lightheartedness enough that you may make sense of this letter. (You may not make sense of it in any case, since the forerunners which explain it are surely still at sea heading in the wrong direction. But Nan can answer most of your questions.)

As you know, Mr. Strickland and I were on the road home by eight o'clock yesterday morning; I thought we did very well for having stopped to say good-by to you and delivering your wife to her new house and housekeeper. In fact I was suddenly so ravenous when we reached that long stretch with no inn that I was rummaging through my reticule in search of a forgotten peppermint lozenge.

"Are you hungry, my love?" Mr. Strickland asked. He had said so little all the morning that I had begun to fear I was never going to be his love.

I nodded in response, not trusting myself to speak.

"I asked the innkeeper in Southampton to pack us a luncheon," he said in so ordinary a tone that I might have imagined the endearment. "Would you like to stop at the copse ahead?"

My reticence was overcome by a combination of his nonchalance and my appetite. "I'm famished," I admitted. "And I was certain luncheon was hours away. A picnic sounds perfect."

We pulled up by the grove of sycamore trees, and Mr. Strickland extracted the luncheon basket from our luggage. He saw to the horses while I unpacked the innkeeper's idea of a roadside repast: fat sandwiches made with slabs of roast, two bottles of wine, and enough apple tart for a houseparty. Please do not think that I found fault with his selections: I don't know when a meal has tasted so good.

"Better now?" Mr. Strickland asked as I used a napkin to wipe away the traces of my second sandwich.

"Oh, yes," I said contentedly, reaching for an apple tart. "Thank you. I'm so glad you thought of it."

"I've been thinking of a lot of things," he said seriously.

I put down my apple tart. "So have I," I answered. "I must thank you for your kindnesses to Nan these last few days. I am sorry for the harsh words to which I subjected you earlier."

"That sounds almost rehearsed," Mr. Strickland commented, a twinkle in his eye.

"Then I obviously did not rehearse it enough," I said peevishly. "It is nonetheless sincere. You could not have done more to help Nan and by extension my whole family. I appreciate it more than I can say." I did not look at him. "Can you not accept my apology?"

"You owe me no apology," he said, reverting to solemnity. "You've given me food for thought. I admit I misjudged your Nan." He paused. "I should say, your brother's Nan. She will make him a fine wife."

I looked up at that, and he hurried on.

"I'm the one who should apologise to you," he said. "I

regret what I said in anger about your mother. It was unfair. Pray forgive me?''

I took a deep breath. ''I've been considering that too,'' I said. ''And I can see how Mama's drinking might look like blackmail. But truly I believe it is not. My mother is not a strong person, and when there is a crisis she misses the comfort and competence she lost when my father died.''

''Yes, I can see that,'' Mr. Strickland concurred. He paused. ''It seems possible that she will soon acquire, by marriage, another protector,'' he said, choosing his words carefully. ''Do you mind?''

''Do you think so?'' I answered quickly. I didn't need to ask whom he meant. ''Nan believes they are fond of each other. Of course I don't mind, if it will bring Mama happiness.'' I remembered that he, too, had a stake in Mr. Rockingham's future. ''Do *you* mind?'' I asked.

''Do you mind, *Giles*?'' he prompted.

''Do you mind, Giles?'' I repeated obediently. I confess my heart began to beat more rapidly.

''Not at all,'' he said immediately. ''You must remember that I also expect to be closely connected to your family.''

I looked at him expectantly and he gestured toward the apple tart in my hand. ''Are you going to eat that?'' he asked.

''There must be a dozen more, if you want one,'' I said puzzled. ''Or are you in a hurry to be on our way?'' I moved the pastry toward my mouth.

''I'm in a hurry to be finished with luncheon,'' Mr. Strickland explained. ''I'd rather not kiss someone who is pondering apple tart.''

''Someone you were kissing would be unlikely to ponder apple tart,'' I said without thinking.

''Let's put it to the test,'' he said. He leaned across the cloth and kissed me lightly on the lips. I dropped the tart to my plate. After a long moment he pulled away a fraction of an inch. "Apple tart?" he asked against my mouth.

"What's that?" I asked from the same distance.

He kissed me once more then, not so lightly, and I may never think about apple tart again. Every cell in my body was warmed by his touch. But I don't need to describe passion to two newlyweds. So I shall slide over the next quarter hour and say only that I have never spent a happier fifteen minutes or ones that made me so impatient for the future.

The sound of a farm wagon approaching on the road broke up our idyll. By the time the cart passed by we were sedately packing up the remains—and all the apple tarts—from our picnic.

"I love you, Lily," Mr. Strickland—Giles—said as he folded up the cloth.

I looked up from replacing the tableware in the basket. "I'm so glad," I said. "I loved you long before I would admit it—even to myself."

The farm wagon was by that time out of sight beyond a curve and Giles took me again in his arms. "We could marry today if you will," he said into my hair. "The special license must seal our troth since your sapphire ring is still at Strathamsford."

I leaned back. "I don't think so," I said, and reached up to stroke his cheek. (I can tell already that I shall be enchanted with marriage; why did nobody ever explain it to me? Or do you need to find the right person before you appreciate its charms?)

"You must marry me," Giles insisted, tightening his embrace. "I won't let you go until you say yes."

"I like it here," I teased. "Maybe I'll keep you guessing a while longer."

"I won't kiss you until you recite after me, "I'll marry you, Giles," he threatened.

"May I kiss you instead?" I asked. I reached up and bent his head so that I could reach his mouth with mine.

"That's not fair," he objected after a thoroughly satisfying interval.

"I'll marry you, Giles," I said, and the thoroughly satisfying interval was repeated.

"But not today," I added, more than a little out of breath.

"Not today?" he repeated. "How soon?"

"I'd like a real wedding," I said. "My brother was married by special license. I've always dreamed of dancing after the ceremony."

"I'll ask Mr. Black to give the first reading of the banns on Sunday," Giles said. "Three weeks should be more than ample time to stage a wedding."

I ignored his casual dismissal of the details of trousseau and ceremony and reception. "But we cannot be married without my brother and his wife," I protested.

"Your brother will be riding out to pick up the mail in three weeks time," Giles announced confidently.

He may be overly optimistic. But in any case Mr. and Mrs. Carlisle are invited to a wedding at the Stratham church on Sunday, November 28, 1813. "Summoned" might be a better word, because I doubt the ceremony will take place without you, and I would not relish telling my husband-to-be that it must be postponed. So you must feel well enough to come home very soon.

We did not set speed records on the rest of our journey home, as you might guess. I feel as if we have already begun to live happily ever after. But I won't bore you with our love story. You have your own.

We arrived at Strathamsford just as dinner was being served. I had time only to splash some water on my face and recomb my hair before joining the family in the dining room. Giles waited for me on the landing and slipped the enormous sapphire on the third finger of my left hand. You would have been amused to see me trying to eat using only my right hand. Fortunately everyone was so full of questions about you—both of you—that no one noticed I was not cutting my capon.

Once Mama was convinced that my brother is thriving under his wife's devoted care, and Mr. Rockingham had exchanged a few private sentences with Giles, and Aunt Charlotte had begun several comments on medical care and secret marriages and Cousin Clarissa had cooed over the romance of it all, Mr. Rockingham glanced at Mama and cleared his throat for our attention.

"Helen and I have an announcement to make," he declared. We all looked up expectantly. "She has agreed to become my wife at Christmastime."

Through the chorus of congratulations Mama turned to me. "I had hoped to tell you first, Liza," she said. "But Dan is eager to make our engagement official. Are you pleased?"

"I'm more than pleased, Mama," I answered, and I got up from my place to hug her at the head of the table. I didn't even try to stifle the laughter of pure happiness that bubbled out.

When I put my arms around Mama, of course my new ring glittered in the candlelight. "What's that?" Clarissa asked at once. "It looks like a sapphire."

"We have an announcement to make as well," Giles said, a smile playing at the corners of his mouth. "Liza and I will be married as soon as the banns can be read."

There was another chorus of congratulations, although perhaps not as heartfelt on the part of Aunt Charlotte and Cousin Clarissa.

Mama gave me an intense scrutiny. "Is this what you want, dear?" she asked.

"Yes, Mama," I said, going over to put my hands on Giles's shoulders. "It is." He turned in his chair to give me a look so full of love that I shall dream of it.

"We must have champagne with our dessert," Mama proclaimed. "We have a great many things to celebrate." Just then Sally came quietly into the dining room and whispered in Mama's ear. Mama laughed. "It looks as if we'll have champagne in place of dessert," she said. "Cook sends word that dessert was planned for four rather than six."

I glanced down at Giles. "We brought home a great quantity of apple tart," I offered. "The innkeeper in Southampton packed a luncheon for us."

"You did not eat any apple tart?" Mama asked.

This time I was careful not to look at my fiancé. "No," I answered. "Giles was in a hurry . . ." I let my voice trail off. He put his hands over mine on his shoulders and squeezed them in memory and anticipation. I'm glad I waited for him before I fell in love.

And so at least four of those at Strathamsford are euphorically happy. Aunt Charlotte and Cousin Clarissa leave shortly to visit friends in London; I don't blame them: no one pays them the slightest attention.

Do hurry and get well enough to travel: you have a wedding to attend.

I must close. Giles is at my side urging me to ride with him. So enough of the past; I am off to my future. Giles sends warm wishes along with

love from
Elizabeth

P.S. And you know? There's not a single conversation here that I wish to revise by as much as a comma.